Not M

Michele L. Rivera

Text copyright © 2018 by Michele L. Rivera
All Rights Reserved
Editor: Jordan F. Summers
First Paperback Edition

Yesterday, I locked away
all of my most breakable parts-
My soul,
My sweetness,
My spirit,
My heart
So that now, I can stand alone
In one piece
Only slightly chipped around the edges
Because nothing is perfect
Painless
Or free
It is what I have learned after everything leaves
After watching stars fall from summer skies
After listening desperately to lies within lies
After mourning the days of a thousand goodbyes
This lock is my never again will I try
You see,
No longer can I be crushed
By a dangerous gaze
A soft kiss
A hot touch
So girl, save your love for someone who believes
One that will ache for you
Cry for you,
Bleed
Go search for another to hold you at night,
To wrap your body around in unspoken delight
One who will fight to bring life to your dreams
Just walk away like the rest; who you seek is not me
Even if maybe I want it to be
Because deep down I know every lock has a key.

Chapter One

Blake

I can feel her gaze on me. Again. *Does she really think I can't see her checking me out? I mean my peripheral vision is on point.* As I take another sip of my drink, I tip my head ever so slightly to my right at the woman in the black button down shirt sitting exactly five barstools away from me with only a patron between us, who has been nursing the same glass of chardonnay for about half an hour now. This is my third attempt to catch Black Button Down in the act of leering. Poor thing doesn't realize she lacks the subtlety necessary to be a successful player. I would know. I'm prepared to give her my renowned look of disgust when she realizes she's been discovered, but the longest layer of her sandy blonde bob covers her face just in time. I internally groan and roll my eyes as I place my drink back on the bar. I read the labels on the bottles on the top shelf behind the bartender, otherwise known as Connor and sigh.

What's the deal with Black Button Down anyway? Does she want me to notice her checking me out? Is this part of her game? Before I can answer my own questions, I hear Connor's voice.

"Compliments of the chick in the black button down to your right." Connor grins as he slides a tall, narrow glass in front of me.

Ah, yes. Part of the game. I eye the new glass of gin and tonic and then look to Connor. "You told her what I was drinking?"

Connor shrugs with his mouth. "Technically, no. She said she'd have what you were having and so that's what I gave her. She's good at this."

I crinkle my brow curiously. "Wait. Do you know her?"

1

Connor chuckles. "Blake, it's a girl bar and I work here every weekend. I know everyone."

"Right," I reply dryly.

"She's cool. You should chat with her."

"No thanks." I gently push the glass to the side. "And tell her I appreciate the gesture but I'm not thirsty."

Connor smirks deviously. "Tell her yourself. She's coming this way." He winks at me and saunters over to the girl who can't seem to finish her wine.

Without warning, Black Button Down's scent hits me. I'm familiar with the notes of vanilla, orange, and sweet cucumber of her perfume. I will myself to keep my focus straight ahead. She creates a small breeze when she sits on the stool next to me. I still don't give her my attention. After a painfully long moment, she speaks.

"Aren't you gonna drink that?" Black Button Down asks, motioning to the glass of gin and tonic on the bar that I've been intentionally neglecting. Her voice is smooth and low.

Let's just get this over with. I slowly turn in my seat to acknowledge Black Button Down and despite myself, I inhale sharply, surprised by her soft features and sparkling white smile. Without shifting my eyes, I appraise her from top to bottom in seconds. Her hair is cut in a sophisticated bob. Up close, I can see the multi-dimensional tones blended throughout her sandy blonde hair; the lighter strands purposely standing out against the darker roots. It's longer and blonder in the front, parted to the left with the longest layer barely above her jawline. Her hair gets shorter towards the back of her head and becomes a bit more of a brown color. The nearly product-free hairstyle compliments her oval-shaped face. Her eyes are crystal blue, but I don't allow myself to view them in detail. Her full bottom lip is pierced on the left side with a fitted hoop. The sleeves of her shirt are rolled up to her elbows, revealing a black tattoo of a star on her right inner forearm. Straight legged jeans. All-white, iconic basketball sneakers. *Could she be more gay?*

I give Black Button Down a weak smile. "No. I wasn't planning on drinking it. But thanks."

Black Button Down frowns. "Why not? Isn't that your drink?"

For fuck's sake. "Nope. It just happens to be what I'm drinking tonight."

A slow grin forms across Black Button Down's lips. "Well it *is* tonight so..."

Can she not take a hint? I clear my throat. "Listen, it was nice of you to buy me a drink, but I'm going to have to decline."

"Are you now?"

I suck in air through my teeth. "Um. Yeah."

"I'm sensing some hostility," Black Button Down says. "Rough day?"

I glare at her. "Alright. I don't want to be mean, but you're obviously really bad at taking hints so I'm just going to ask you to please leave me alone."

Black Button Down nods. "Huh. Okay, but do you mind if I still sit here?"

"Knock yourself out," I say and swivel in my stool to face forward again. I pull my phone from the back pocket of my jeggings to see if I have any missed texts from Grace. Nothing. *Come on, Grace, hurry the hell up.* I don't even have time to flag down Connor for a glass of water before Black Button Down tries to strike up a conversation with me again.

"I'm Hayden."

I don't look at her. I refuse to give her the satisfaction. I nod. "Good for you."

"That was sort of rude," Hayden says. "I'll explain. Typically, the way this goes is that you tell me your name

3

now."

I let out a low growl and turn to Hayden. "Hayden you said?"

Hayden gives me a sideways smile. "That's right."

"Mmm. Okay, *Hayden*, you seem like a decent person so I'm gonna level with you." I scrunch up my face in feigned sympathy. "You're wasting your time here."

Hayden cocks her head to the left, carefully studying my expression. "Why's that?"

"You're not my type," I say matter of factly.

Hayden's eyes widen. "Whoa. You're awfully confident."

I gasp. "Excuse me?"

"Here I am, trying to make friendly conversation and you assume I'm hitting on you."

I snort. "That's because you *are* hitting on me and you're failing miserably."

Hayden purses her lips. "Fine. Maybe I was hitting on you." She shifts in her seat. "Why am I failing?"

I fight back a smile at the sincerity of her question. "First of all, you ogled me for about forty-five minutes before making a move and your actual move was sending over a drink...I mean, really? A drink."

Hayden's shoulders straighten and she holds up her index finger. "Hey. Sending someone a drink is an act of kindness."

"Pshaw. I disagree. *Especially* since that was supposedly your move. So unoriginal."

"And you're some kind of expert on move-making?"
I raise a skeptical eyebrow. "That's not what I said."

"But it's what you're implying."

"Take it how you will."

"Are you always this standoffish?" Hayden asks me.

I tilt my head back and let out a short laugh. "Christ!

You don't even know me."

Hayden places her hand on the bar inches from mine. "Then why don't you give me the privilege of getting to know you?"

"No. I'm all set."

Hayden presses her lips together. "Alright." She points to the untouched gin and tonic she bought me. "How about you give that drink a chance and I'll keep you company. If you still want to hate on me once you've finished, I'll go away and you'll never have to see me again?"

"*Or* I could not drink the drink and you can go away," I retort.

"Where's the fun in that?"

Now I understand. "Ahh. I get it. You get off on challenges, yes?"

Hayden gapes in mock disbelief. "Whaaat?! Christ! You don't even know me." She expertly mimics me from earlier. I cave in and smile.

"Fine," I say. "If you can refrain from trying to hit on me, I'll engage in small talk with you."

"Deal." Hayden grins. "So, do you come here often?"

Welp that was a bust. "Oh my god! Did you seriously just use one of the most hackneyed pick-up lines on me?" I clench my fists. "Literally a millisecond after I specifically told you not to hit on me no less."

Hayden cringes. "No. No. No. That's not what I meant. I didn't mean for it to sound like...ugh." She shakes her head. "I didn't mean for the question to sound like a pick-up line. It was a genuine inquiry."

"Riiight."

"Well do you?"

I shoot Hayden a look that lets her know I'm very close to planning her death. "You had one shot and you blew it."

"False. You misunderstood me therefore you can't hold me accountable. That's not fair."

"Okay. I'll answer your stupid question and then we're done."

Hayden shakes her head. "I'm sorry but that would go against the terms and conditions of our arrangement and I can't let that happen."

I clench my jaw. "Our arrangement?"

"Yup. You drink and we small talk. That was the arrangement," Hayden practically chirps.

Well I am bored and I have to kill time somehow until I get a text from Grace. Reluctantly, I wrap my hand around the sweaty glass and take a sip of the gin and tonic. "Okay. I'll uphold the arrangement, but only because you're like obsessed with me and I feel sorry for you."

"Ha! I'm not obsessed with you."

I shrug. "If you say so."

Hayden narrows her eyebrows. "I think you're messing with me." She nods. "Fine. That's fine. So I'll ask you again, do you come here often?"

"Not particularly. I don't do clubs and bars. They're not my thing."

Hayden glances around the dimly lit establishment. Eighties pop music is pounding through the speakers by the dancefloor, but it's not loud enough to infiltrate any conversations taking place by the wide, circular booths, the few high-top tables, or the bar, where I'm currently sitting with Hayden. The seating area is mostly occupied and the dancefloor is crowded with queer girls ranging between the ages of twenty-one and forty, which is typical for a Friday night here at Luscious. Finally, Hayden's eyes find my face again. "So why is it your thing tonight?"

"Why do you ask so many questions?"

"I'm an inquisitive creature."

I roll my eyes. "You're annoying as fuck is what you are." I take another drink. "I'm here as wing woman for my best friend."

Hayden looks around. "So where is she?"

"She's probably hooking up with someone in the bathroom."

Hayden chuckles. "It doesn't seem like she is in need of wing woman then."

"Well, you don't know her. She has terrible taste in women and too much of a taste for alcohol. I'm here to keep her in line."

"How? If she's having sexy time in the bathroom and you're out here at the bar, how are you keeping her in line?" Hayden asks.

I wince. "Sexy time? Yikes. No wonder you were all alone. Also, I resent your air quotes. I am keeping her in line. *I* picked out the girl she's with."

"All the more reason for me to be frightened for her and I don't even know her."

"Fuck you."

Hayden bites her bottom lip as her eyes blatantly roam my body. "Mmm. If only I were your type."

"Yeah. If only but you're not," I say. "Moving on. What's your story?" I quickly hold my hand up in front of her mouth. "Wait! Let me guess."

"Go for it."

I rest my hand back on my lap. "You're a regular here. You sit in that same stool every weekend, creep on all the girls and when you find one you think will fall for your pathetic antics, you approach her-possibly after forty-five minutes-then you take her home—probably her home, not yours— and call it a night."

Hayden nods approvingly. "Impressive."

I smile. "I'm good at reading people."

7

"It would seem so." Hayden crosses her arms over her chest. "Since you know everything about me now, how about you at least tell me your name?"

"Psht. No. Nice try though."

"Oh. C'mon. I told you my name," Hayden says.

"Yes, but I didn't ask for it. You offered it up. Not my problem."

Hayden pouts. "Then what should I call you?"

I exhale deeply. "You don't call me anything because once this small talk thing is done with, you're going to go your way and I'm going to go mine and that's the end of it."

"Wow. Cynical much?"

"No. More of a realist."

"For all you know, we could become best friends for life." Hayden gives me her grin again.

"I have a best friend already."

"As do I, but you can never have too many friends. Am I right?"

I shake my head. "You are wrong."

"Fine. Don't tell me your name. Have lunch with me tomorrow," Hayden proposes.

I nearly choke on the gin and tonic making its way down my throat. I cough. "What? Are you crazy? I won't even give you my name. What the hell makes you think I'll go out with you? Besides—"

"I'm not your type," Hayden interrupts me. "Don't worry. I didn't forget, but I'm not asking you on a date. I'm asking you to have lunch with me."

"Uh huh. And the difference between the two is what?" I stare at her expectantly.

"Friends have lunch and we're becoming friends," Hayden explains.

"No. We are not." *What is her damage?*

"But we could be."

"Dude, what is your problem? Do you really think this is going to work?" I ask.

"If what's going to work?"

I press my fist against my forehead. "That you'll take me to lunch and suddenly I'll change my mind and decide to go to bed with you."

"Whoa. Calm down, Oh-Cynical-One. Your arrogance is showing and to be honest, it's not a flattering look on you."

I give up. "What on earth do you want from me?"

"I want to take you to lunch to get to know you and maybe even learn your name." Hayden's tone is thick with innocence. I remain wary of her.

"That's all? You want to get acquainted with me and nothing else?"

"Correct. I'm strictly seeking a friendship. Aside from that, I don't expect anything in return."

"I call bullshit. Everybody wants something."

Hayden's expression sobers. "I disagree."

"Agree. Disagree. I don't care."

"Damn. You've got issues," Hayden says.

I laugh. I didn't mean to, but I did. *Shit.* I recover quickly. "You have no idea."

"Well, if you'd let me be your friend, I'm an excellent listener."

I glance to the left and Connor is staring at us, snickering as he cleans a glass with the white cloth that's usually draped over his shoulder. I mentally flip him off. Then I look at Hayden. "I'll pass."

"You know, you're rather hostile." Hayden nods along with her statement. "How do you even survive socially?"

"Nowadays, no one has to be *that* social to survive thanks to the internet and mobile apps," I say. I realize way too late that I've given Hayden more information than I ever intended to. I cringe on the inside. Much to my astonishment, Hayden doesn't have an opposing reaction to this new intel. However, there's a pregnant pause between us as she digests my words.

"Alright then," Hayden starts. "We can go to lunch and you can sit in silence and I'll do all the talking."

"Isn't that what's happening right now?" I quip.

Hayden runs her hand over her face. "You win. No lunch, but will you please tell me your name?"

"What for?" I ask.

"It'll come in handy when I go to stalk you on the internet."

There it is.

I stare at Hayden gravely. "That's not funny. There are real victims of cyber stalking and cyber bullying. All sorts of shit. And you're sitting here joking about it? What kind of animal are you?"

Hayden flinches as the color drains from her face. I'm only half-serious but she doesn't need to know that.

"I...I'm sorry," Hayden says softly.

I crack a smile and Hayden's mouth drops open.

"That was totally mean," Hayden accuses.

"And yet, I'm not even sorry about it." I take the last sip of my gin and tonic.

Hayden returns my smile. "C'mon. What's a girl gotta do to get your name?"

"She has to have a better game than yours."

"Oh snap!" Hayden legitimately snaps her fingers. "No, but really?"

I chuckle. I have to give Hayden credit for her persistence. It's almost admirable. I open my mouth to say my name when my phone vibrates. I glance down at the screen. It's a text from Grace, who is finally ready to emerge the bathroom and go home. *Thank the Gods!* I hop off my stool and wave my phone in front of Hayden's face.

"I gotta go," I say. "Thanks for the drink."

Hayden gets out of her seat so that we're both standing. "You're leaving?"

"That's what I said."

"Maybe you can meet up with me next Friday and we can hang out...as friends?" Hayden suggests hastily as I place a few dollar bills on the bar for Connor and gather my belongings. "I'd like to...it would be cool to see you again sometime."

I furnish a tight-lipped smile. "Take care, Hayden. Polish up your game." I begin to walk away.

"Yeah. Sure," Hayden's voice trails me. "Take care..."

I slowly come to a stop and turn around. Hayden's staring at me. "Blake." I finish her sentence, quickly change my direction back towards the exit, and leave.

Chapter Two

Hayden

"Hello!" I call into the dark, seemingly empty two-bedroom apartment I refer to as home. I've lived here for almost five years now with my best friend slash roommate, Ava. I close the door and flip the switch to lock it. The entrance is basically in the small kitchen of our digs, where the oven light remains on because we've yet to replace our broken nightlight. I hang my keys on the key rack that Ava insisted we get for "organizational purposes," and step quietly through the kitchen towards the living room. I plop down on the sofa and lean forward to take off my sneakers.

"Someone's home early for a Friday night." Ava's voice pierces the quietness of the room.

I smile to myself as I sit up and turn to the direction of Ava's bedroom on the right side of the living room. "Hey. I thought you might be sleeping."

Ava's in her pink flannel pajama shorts and a matching, fitted tank top that rises slightly above her belly button. *Stop staring.*

"Nope. I've been up doing research," Ava says.

My forehead creases. "Research? On a Friday night? Why?"

Ava releases a long, deep exhale as she begins to trudge towards me. When she's about a foot away from the sofa, she switches on the tall floor lamp in the corner of the room. Eventually she reaches her destination and curls up on the last cushion of the couch. She wraps her arms around her bent knees in such a way that I can see up her shorts a little. Enough to make out the edge of her panties. *Stop staring.*

"The principal approached me at the end of the day to inform me that a faculty member caught two students after school in the girls' bathroom...with pills," Ava explains.

"Apparently they claimed that the pills didn't belong to them; the girls said they found them in a stall so they were let off with a warning. But now I have a meeting Monday morning with these kids and their parents. We're going over the school's drug-free policy and discussing substance abuse and addiction to make sure everyone is informed and on the same page." Ava takes a deep breath. "So I've been carefully reviewing the school's policies and scraping together as many resources as I possibly can because if they do have a problem, I...I want to be prepared." Ava hugs her legs closer to her body. "The whole thing has me stressed out. Like I'm not naïve, I know some of the students probably use based on statistics alone, but now that it's in my face and very much a reality, I'm legitimately worried."

I nod. Ava shifts in her seat and eyes me carefully. "Did I trigger you?"

I realize I'd been fidgeting with one of the three hoops in my right ear. I casually lower my arm and fold my hands on my lap. "What? No. I'm alright."

"Do you want me to stop talking about it?"

"No." I shake my head as I lean sideways into my own cushion so that I can face my best friend. "Aves, really. I'm fine. You can keep talking."

Ava chews on her thumbnail briefly and then continues. "It's part of my job to make sure these kids feel safe at school...and that they *are* safe at school. It's only the second week of September. The students at Samson Prep are between fourteen and eighteen years old and they're getting drunk and getting high and it's like everyone is turning a blind eye to it. It fucking pisses me off. I want to do something that really encourages the school as a whole to implement earlier intervention and to provide these kids with a more comprehensive education about substances because clearly health class and the lecture we give on the dangers of drugs once a goddamn year aren't cutting it." Ava sighs again. "I'm sorry for venting."

"You don't have to apologize."

"I'm putting together a presentation for our next staff meeting. I need to do this...for the students and for..." Ava pauses and frowns.

"Ava." I offer her a small smile. "I think it's amazing what you're doing and if you believe that it's something you should do then you absolutely should do it, but you don't have to do it for me. You don't owe me anything."

"But you're my best friend."

"And you're mine," I say.

"I just want to help."

"Then all you have to do is keep being my best friend." I smirk. "Okay?"

Ava smiles back at me with her eyes, the bright blue of her irises shine even in the barely lit room. "Okay."

"Permission to change the subject?"

Ava nods. "Permission granted."

"How was your post-work coffee date today with what's-his-face?"

"His face is Jacob and it sucked."

I pout. "I'm sorry."

"No worries," Ava says and then she narrows her gaze. "You never told me why you got home so early. You hardly ever come home before midnight on the weekends. What's up with that?"

I wince. "Yeah. I kinda struck out."

Ava gasps dramatically. "Nooooo. Say it ain't so."

I chuckle. "I did. I struck out hard."

"Bummer. How's your ego?"

"What do you think? It's destroyed!" I place the back of my hand on my forehead theatrically. "Shattered into a

14

million pieces. The damage is irreparable."

Ava giggles. "Aww. Will ice cream ease your woes?"

"It depends on the flavor."

"Mocha chip."

I grin. "No harm in trying."

Ava gets up from the sofa and starts walking towards the kitchen. "I heard a rumor that scotch pairs awesomely with ice cream," she announces excitedly to my backside.

"We should totally find out if there's any truth to that." I crane my neck to check out Ava as she evenly distributes scoops of ice cream into two small ceramic bowls. After a long second, I unwillingly peel my gaze away from her and rise from my seat. "I'll get the drinks."

Within minutes, Ava and I are back on the sofa, sitting cross-legged on our respective cushions, facing one another. We're each cupping our ice cream bowls while our glasses of scotch await us on the coffee table situated in front of the couch.

"Your turn. Tell me how this strike out of yours went down," Ava demands.

I eat another spoonful of ice cream to bide my time before discussing my night's defeat. I swallow and shake my head. "It's nothing really. Just some chick at Luscious who acted like she was the Universe's gift to womankind."

Ava finishes off her ice cream and places her bowl on the table. She picks up one of the glasses of scotch and takes a sip. "Was she cute?"

Fuck yeah! "Meh. She was alright."

Ava laughs. "Liar! You sooo thought she was cute. I saw it in your eyes. You're SUCH an easy read."

I inwardly grimace. "You saw no such thing."

"Oh. I saw." Ava smiles broadly. "What did she look like?"

I take my last bite of ice cream and trade the empty

bowl for my glass of scotch. Unlike Ava, I take a greedy drink from my glass. I wait for the warmth of the alcohol to flow through my bloodstream before I speak. "Why do you want to know what she looks like?"

"Because I'm human and because I'm a visual learner," Ava responds. "Plus, I want to know what I'm up against." She winks at me. *Good God.* My stomach flies away. Luckily, I've had years of practice acting collected in moments like this one.

"There is no competition when it comes to you," I say, coolly.

"You're sweet."

"You're sweeter."

Ava smiles. "Alright, Don Juan, Quit stalling. Gimme the deets."

I attempt to redirect the conversation as if I didn't hear Ava. "You know, I was wondering if you've ever considered meeting people online or using one of those dating apps?"

"Hayden!" My best friend chastises me.

"Seriously though. You're always talking about how your dating life is a disaster but you only date people you've met through other people or those speed dating events you attend for whatever reason. I'm not judging. But maybe you should try a different approach."

Ava cringes. "No thank you. Talking to people without ever having met them in person weirds me out. Have you never heard of catfishing?"

I chuckle. "Of course I have, but I'd help you if it's something you wanted to experiment with. You hate going out and thus far, your current methods have proven to be ineffectual so this could be a loophole."

"I don't think so, Hayden."

"Just mull it over. I have an informant who apparently

swears by it."

"An informant?" Ava asks suspiciously. "Who?"

"The chick who rejected me."

Ava raises an eyebrow at me. "No way."

"Yes way."

"And the plot thickens."

"Aves, have you not been paying attention? The plot doesn't even exist. I'm only saying that this chick's all about it. Maybe you could be all about it too."

"No."

"Think about it."

"No."

I bat my lashes playfully. "Pleeease. Please. Please. Please."

"Ugh. Fine. I'll *maybe* think about it."

I clap victoriously. "Nice!"

"*M-a-y-b-e*," Ava repeats slowly. Then she clears her throat. Her expression turns serious. "Okay. Now you do something for me."

Oh boy. "What?"

"Stop keeping me in suspense. What did she look like?"

I run my thumb over my chin to appear as though I'm delving into the recesses of my mind to conjure up the image of Blake, but I'm not. I haven't stopped thinking about her since she walked away from me.

Killer cognac-brown eyes. Long lashes embellished with just the right amount of mascara. Nearly flawless olive complexion. Small diamond stud in her left nostril. Slightly wavy, layered, chocolate brown hair falling a little past her shoulder blades. Magnetizing smile. *That smile.* Thick, tantalizing lips painted with barely-there tinted gloss. Short manicured fingernails. Hourglass figure bedecked in light colored jeggings, a long white tee shirt, partially tucked in

17

beneath an open navy blue blazer. Tall leather boots with flat bottoms. *So freaking sexy.*

I meet Ava's anticipative stare. "I don't remember."

Ava's mouth drops. "You're such a bad liar so just don't!"

"Aargh. I'd really rather not relive the humiliation of being rejected. I'm begging you."

Ava simpers at me.

"What?" I ask.

"Oh please. You've been rejected before."

"Thanks for reminding me."

"Shoosh! Let me finish," Ava says. "I'm going somewhere with this. My point is, when you've been rejected in the past, you move on right away like it's no big deal. But you're not moving on. It's bugging you this time. This one is different than the others. She got under your skin."

I rub the back of my neck. "Yeah. A little but that's because…" I struggle to formulate an explanation. *Fuck. Why did she get to me?* I half-shrug. "She was intriguing."

"In what way?" Ava inquires.

"In an interesting way."

"Mmhmm. Can you expand on that?"

I sigh. "Well she outright rejected me, but then she let me sit next to her and we talked. Who does that? Who rejects someone only to engage with them afterwards? I'll tell you who does that…no one. Nobody does that. She definitely had her guard up but there was this thing about her and I'm not even sure what it was, but a part of me wanted to find out what was under her guard." I can *hear* myself babbling and I want to smack myself across the face.

Ava squints at me. "Is that your way of saying you wanted to find out what was under her clothes?"

"No," I say firmly though I'm one thousand percent not opposed to that. I immediately feel the tips of my ears

18

burning. *Great.*

Ava raises her arm in the air and lets out a big laugh. "Oh my gosh! Your ears! Youuu have a crush on her!"

No I don't! "What?! No I don't!" I flex my jaw to keep myself from telling Ava why she is wrong.

"Hayden, you actually wanted to make a non-physical connection with her. That's huge!"

"No! Stop! It's not huge. It's like so...microscopic."

Ava reaches out and clutches my left shoulder. "Denial is normal." She giggles.

I brush Ava's hand away. "I'm serious. I don't have a crush on her. I just..." I blank. *I just what? Think!* "It was refreshing to talk to someone without an end game." I nod. *That's good. Go with that. It's the ONLY logical reasoning for all of this.* "It was like having a friend...albeit a semi-bitchy one, but still."

Ava shoots me a dubious look. "You really don't think there's a crush happening here?"

"Nope. No crushing."

"Okay then. What do I know?" Ava holds up her arms, surrendering.

You have no idea.

Ava and I sit in silence for a couple of seconds and then she speaks again. "Well, it'll be good for you to have another friend aside from me."

I gape. "You make it seem as though I have no friends."

Ava winces. "Um. That's because you don't. You keep to yourself. A lot."

I stick my tongue out at Ava. We both know she's right. "It doesn't matter if it would be good for me or not, she wasn't interested in having a friendship with me either."

"Why not?"

"Beats me. When she left, she left. No phone number. Nothing. And I'll probably never see her again because she gave me a very strong impression that she doesn't want to be seen...not by me."

The corners of Ava's mouth curl up in a devilish grin.

"Did you get her name?"

"Mmm Mmm. No. Why are you wearing that creepy smile?"

"Calm yourself," Ava says. "Did you get her name?"

"I might've. Why?"

"You said she's plugged in. If you have her name then maybe we can find her online. Like spies."

I think back to my conversation with Blake and suppress a laugh. "You mean like stalkers?"

"Pfft. No. It's simply playing detective."

"Nah. It's cool. I don't wanna," I say.

"Come on. Everybody does it."

"Dude, quit it with the peer pressure."

"Alright. Chill." Ava kicks my leg sportively. "*You* don't have to. *I* will. Heh? How's that?"

"What would be the point?" I ask. "She doesn't want anything to do with me."

"Then I'll do it for shits and giggles because now *I'm* super curious about who this person is that's got you all frazzled."

"I'm not frazzled."

"Sure you're not." Ava stares at me wide-eyed. "Her name?"

I groan. "Whatever information you uncover, I don't want to know about it."

"Okay."

"Promise?" I hold out my pinky to Ava.

"I promise." Ava wraps her pinky around mine.

I'm suddenly extremely aware of how fast my heart is

beating. *Why am I nervous?* I casually pull my hand back from Ava's grip. That should have regulated my heart rate but it didn't. *Why?* Ava's looking at me eagerly. I exhale slowly. "Her name is Blake." Instantly, my stomach flips over itself. *What in the hell was that?*

Chapter Three

Blake

I walk over to the loveseat in the center of the living room of my two-bedroom condominium and place a steaming cup of coffee, glass of water and bottle of aspirin on the end table. I reach down and give Grace's sprawled out body a light shake. She groans and pulls the throw blanket I covered her with last night up over her face, blocking out the sun that's streaming through the sliding windows.

"Rise and shine," I say indifferently.

Grace bemoans again. I stand up straight. "You have to get up, Grace." I put my hands on my hips. "I have to leave for work soon or I'll be late."

Grace pushes the blanket off herself and sits up slowly. She presses her palm against her forehead. "Oh man."

"Yeah. I figured you'd be greeted with a hangover this morning," I say. "I put your go-to remedy on the table."

Grace turns a little and takes the aspirin and water from the table. She glances up at me. "Thanks."

"You're welcome. Now hurry up and get a move on."

"Wait. Why am I here?" Grace asks. "Why didn't you just drop me off at my house?"

I snort. "You were barely conscious. I didn't feel right leaving you alone in that state."

"Awe. You're sweet."

I roll my eyes and point to the items in her hands. "Take your medicine and let's go. I'll give you a lift home on my way."

"I don't remember much after I came out of the bathroom at Luscious."

"Shocker."

"What I *do* remember is that the girl you introduced

22

me to had stamina. I mean...wow." Grace grins.

"I'm glad you had fun."

"Did you meet anyone?"

Before I can get a handle on my thoughts, I picture Hayden. *That ridiculously perfect smile. God, she was annoying.* I shrug. "I talked to someone at the bar but that was the extent of it."

"You weren't in the mood to hook up?" Grace asks.

"Not with her."

Grace nods as she places the glass of water and bottle of pain reliever back on the table and begins to put on her shoes. "What was wrong with her?"

I shake my head. "She wasn't my type."

At that, Grace knows not to push the issue any further. She finishes getting herself ready, takes a few sips of the coffee I made and uses the armrest of the loveseat to maneuver herself out of the two-seater couch and onto her feet. "Okay. Let's hit the road. What time are you working until?"

"I have to close tonight so I won't get home until about eleven thirty-ish."

Grace's expression contorts into one of disgust. "Ugh. I don't know how you work in retail."

I grab my purse, keys and cellphone from the island in the kitchen as I head towards the front door with Grace at my heels. "The money's good."

"Ha! Yeah because you're like a super badass boss bitch."

Once Grace and I are both in the hallway, I close and lock the door to my place. I turn to my best friend. "You mean store manager and really, you're too kind with the flattery."

"Right. That's what I meant," Grace says sarcastically.

We step out of the condominium complex and into

the bright September morning. The chill in the air is a reminder that fall is fast approaching. *I fucking hate the cold.* I pull my sunglasses from my purse and put them on as Grace follows me to my car.

"You know what I don't understand?" Grace asks as she opens the passenger side door to my black sedan.

No. And I honestly don't care. "What?" I ask as I slide behind the steering wheel.

Grace fastens her seatbelt. "You work in a high-end lingerie store. You see shit tons of women all day and all night long. Some of them *have* to be queer because…one in ten. Why don't you hit on them? Why are you so hell-bent on using websites and apps?"

I start the engine. "Are you really trying to have this conversation with me again?"

"Yup."

I back out of my parking space and drive slowly towards the exit of the garage and onto the long stretch of road in the center of town. "Alright. Listen closely because this is the last time I'm going to explain this to you. I don't mix business with pleasure for one and second, the whole let-me-woo-you-in-person thing does nothing for me. It's too… personal." I curl my upper lip. "Blech."

Grace chuckles. "Because being behind a screen of some sort protects you? Makes you feel less vulnerable?"

"Yes. That's exactly why."

"Honey, you're twenty-nine. Don't you think you should practice letting your guard down so that you can make genuine connections?"

"I know how old I am, thanks. And I'm pretty content with the superficial connections I'm making and how I'm making them so please take your life-coachy recommendations and shove them up your ass. M'kay?"

Grace gasps. "Um. I believe you meant to tell me to

24

shove them up my incredibly *firm yet shapely* ass. Do you think I go to spin class because it's fun? No."

I laugh and Grace joins in. "Look, I'm not like you," I say.

"What am I like?"

"You know. You're into romance and love and you want to share your life with someone. That's not me."

"It could be you," Grace says.

I scoff. "I don't want it to be me. That's the whole point."

I pull over as we near Grace's apartment. Once the car is stopped, I look at Grace. "Fix your face. What's with the frown?"

"I'm sad. I feel sad for you, Blake. You're going to grow old alone and I won't be around to take care of you because I'll be living on an island far, far away from this place with my hot wife, orgasming from here to eternity," Grace says.

I raise an eyebrow at her, but fail at suppressing my smile. "Wow. You've got it all planned out, haven't you?"

"I do."

"And there's nothing unrealistic about your expectations. That's remarkable," I deadpan.

"Hey. I was taught to dream big and so I do."

I press my lips together. "Yeah. Good luck with that."

Grace gives me the middle finger. "You watch."

I flip her off in return. "Go take a shower. You reek of tequila."

Grace holds up her other middle finger. "Think about I said while you're at work today amidst an abundance of women."

I lower my middle finger and then raise it again with more emphasis. "I won't."

Grace opens the passenger door and gets out. She

pokes her head inside the vehicle. "Bitch," she mutters.
"Skank."

Grace smirks. "Thanks for taking care of me."

"Sure."

"Buttface," she says quickly and shuts the door.

"Douchebag!" I holler and drive off.

I pass through the entrance of Quincy Plaza at 7:30 a.m. and opt for the stairs over the escalator to the second floor where Undercover is located. The mall corridors are mostly deserted save for the small population of folks who enjoy walking around the plaza for exercise. The stores in the mall don't officially open for business until ten o' clock in the morning, but I like to be in early to prepare for the day before my crew arrives for the first shift. I take a sip of my iced quad espresso and unlock the gate to the store.

By the time I hang my jean jacket in my locker, log into the company's computer system, review yesterday's data, and audit the inventory shipment we received, I'm left with twenty minutes until Kendall and Julie get here. I lean back in the leather chair behind the desk in the small office at the rear of the store. I slip my phone from the front pocket of my skinny jeans and swipe on the dating app "Tap That." I have nine new notifications from users who took an interest in my profile. I skim the messages but give a brief response to only one of them. I close the app, finish my drink, shut my phone off and secure it in my locker.

Just as I step out of the office, Julie and Kendall are making their way into the store. The girls wave to me and I greet them back with a stiff smile as I walk towards them to explain to them what the current sales goals are and how I want the latest display laid out. I have about a fourteen hour shift ahead of me and I intend to bust my ass for the entirety of it. I'm completely focused on getting all of my tasks done whilst maintaining our store's number one ranking in the district that is until I pass by the perfume counter and get a whiff of our signature fragrance, Sorcery by Undercover.

Unexpectedly, I lose my breath and stop in my tracks as if the smell is holding me in place. *The fuck?* I've been smelling this perfume since its release last month. It's never had an effect on me. Ever. *Why now?* I inhale again and suddenly I'm back at the bar and I can smell her. It's Hayden's smell. *Fuck my life.*

"Blake?" Kendall's voice pulls me from my thoughts, which I'm grateful for because obviously I'm suffering from some kind of trauma. *Thanks a lot, Hayden.*

I turn to Kendall. "Yeah?"

"Um. Are you okay?"

"Me? What? Yes. I'm fine."

Kendall nods. "Alright. You looked kinda spooked is all."

Accurate. I shake my head. "No. I'm good." I mentally bitch slap myself. *You're good. Let it go.*

Chapter Four

Hayden

"Dude, you need a new set of wheels. Stat," Ava says to me as I cut the engine to my car.

I frown and place my hand on the dashboard. "Shh. Don't say that in front of her."

Ava rolls her eyes. "Seriously. You're thirty and good-looking."

I grin. "Why thank you."

"I'm not done," Ava says. "And you drive a station wagon." Ava shakes head. "A station wagon, Hayden. So not sexy."

I run my other hand over the steering wheel. "Don't listen to her, Leela, she doesn't mean it," I say to my vehicle.

Ava grabs the wheel. "Yes, Leela, I do mean it." She looks at me. "I know you're fond of your first car EVER but the time has come to retire her."

"Psht. What do you know about cars? Nothing."

"I know that she putts around like she's dying and that 1989 sent out a group text saying they want their station wagon returned to them." Ava cracks up laughing at her own joke.

"Actually, she was born in 1991. See? You don't even know her," I say. "And she only putts when I go to park her. She's not dying."

"She is."

"She's not. She just needs an oil change." I bite my bottom lip. "And a transmission flush." I lower my eyes. "And a tire rotation."

"Mhmm."

"Leela and I have been through a lot together, and I'm not ready to give her up," I explain.

"Welp if you ask me, you're insulting the real Leela Clementine. Defiling her name and shit."

"But I didn't ask you." I take my keys out of the ignition, unfasten my seatbelt, and open my door. "Leela stays. Now can we get this over with?"

Ava steps out of my car and turns to her right to take in the four-story mall at the other end of the parking lot. She smiles widely and looks at me. "Why do you hate shopping so much?"

"I don't hate shopping. I just hate *this* mall."

"Why? It's the best mall within a fifty-mile radius of us."

"It's too big and too crowded."

"And you think that the shantytown Liberty Galleria you frequent is better?" Ava challenges me.

"Shopping local is beneficial for the economy."

"Puh-leeze! You just know that the odds of running into one of your no-strings-attached survivors are against you here."

"Well, yeah."

"Don't pay them any mind," Ava says. "Focus on the potentials."

"No way. I'm not here to find a date. I'm here because you begged me to tag along *and* you promised to buy me Pad Thai for lunch." *And because it's the only way to spend time with you.*

"Alright then. Let's get our shop on!" Ava practically cheers.

I groan, defeated, and shove my keys into the pocket of my men's tapered-leg sweatpants. I straighten the flat bill of my snapback and start slogging towards the Quincy Plaza. Ava links arms with me and practically skips in the direction of the mall, pulling me along with her. My stubborn disposition caves at the sight of her enthusiasm. *Le sigh.* "Ugh." I pretend to resist. "Tell me again why you wanted to go shopping today."

"Fall clothing lines!"

"Yay," I mumble.

As Ava and I enter the plaza, I'm immediately overwhelmed by the bright lights and the loud laughter emanating from multiple large groups of teenagers. Ava ushers me over to the mall directory in the center of the first level. She carefully traces the map with her index finger and then taps on a specific location.

"There!" Ava announces. "That's our first destination."

I nod in compliance. "Where is 'there'?"

"Undercover. It's on the second floor." Ava points to the escalators. "Shall we?"

"Um. We shan't. You know I have a fear of escalators." I speak softly to keep any passersby from overhearing my secret.

Recognition registers in Ava's eyes. "Ohh. Right. It's cool. We'll take the stairs then." She grabs my hand and tows me towards the wide staircase at the far end of the first floor. I instantly no longer care where Ava's taking me. I only care about the fact that we're holding hands. *We're like a couple!*

All of a sudden, we come to a stop and Ava frees my hand from hers. I fight the urge to frown. I have no recollection of climbing the stairs or navigating the second floor. I glance down at my empty hand and then look up to see what Ava's staring at. A pink sign with cursive, glittering, white letters that reads: Undercover. Automatically, I step back.

"No. No. No." I shake my head adamantly. "I am not going into some kinky undergarments store. Nope."

Ava turns to me and rolls her eyes. "It's a retailer of

premium womenswear. Not a sex toy shop."

"Still. It's all lacy and frilly...and pink."

Ava chuckles. "I hate to be the bearer of bad news but that perfume I got you for your birthday that you're wearing..."

I raise my arms a little, palms up, confused. "What about it?"

"This is where I got it." Ava's smirking now. "Sorcery by Undercover. Ring any bells?"

I quickly visualize the bottle of perfume on my dresser and the words etched across it. *Fuck me.* Ava's right. I scrunch up my face. "Damnit, Aves. Why you gotta do me like that?"

Ava arches an eyebrow me at me. "Because I knew that if you knew it came from a 'girly' store, you'd never give it a chance. But you didn't know and you wear that shit every day." She grins.

"Ignorance is bliss," I mutter because I have no defense.

"We both know that's not always the case," Ava says. "And furthermore, for an open-minded person, you're really judgmental when it comes to stores. It's unnecessary and kind of immature. Work on that."

I can't lie. I get slightly turned on when Ava calls me out and basically commands me to better myself.
"Yes, Ma'am." I salute.

Ava squints at me. "Don't be facetious."

"Never would I ever even dream of it."

"The hell you wouldn't." Ava gestures to Undercover's entryway. "Let's go then," she says and starts for the store.

I brace myself and hesitantly follow my best friend.

The inside of Undercover is somewhat dim. The walls are dark pink, decorated with photographs of scantily clad models. Not that I'm complaining. There's a familiar pop song resounding through the speakers. I'm surrounded by tables covered with various styles of underwear, bras, and lingerie. I'm very much not in my element. I turn my eyes away from the display of thongs in search of Ava, but the store is long and she's nowhere in sight. Probably in the dressing room in which case I should go to her to offer my opinion about anything she may be trying on. I smile to myself and begin walking through the store towards the fitting rooms in the back, careful not to bump into any of the partially-nude mannequins or other shoppers.

Unexpectedly, all of my attention falls onto a tall black and white picture on the wall to my right of a woman sprawled across a leather sofa wearing a garter belt fastened to sheer mesh thigh highs, a lace-embellished demi bra, a bowtie, and high heels. My body temperature rises. *I'm so gay.*

"Excuse me. Is there something I can help you with?" A voice asks from behind me.

My breath ceases. *I recognize that voice.* I swallow what feels like a mouthful of sand and turn around slowly to face her. I hear her quiet gasp, which she tries to conceal by clearing her throat. I can't help but smile.

Chapter Five

Blake

Are you fucking kidding me?! Of course she's here. Of course this is my life. Okay, breathe. I clear my throat. *Now what the fuck is she smiling about?! Grr!*

"Hayden?" I try to maintain a steady voice.

"Blake. Hi."

I press my lips together. "You really were serious about stalking me, weren't you?"

Hayden's smile disappears and her mouth drops. "What? No!"

"No? Then it's a coincidence that you just so happened to show up at my *job* the day after you meet me and find out my name, is that it?" I will myself to stay composed so as not to draw any attention my way. After all, I *am* a professional.

Hayden holds up both of her hands as if to fend me off. "Whoa. Whoa. You work here?" Her eyes move from my face to the name badge hanging around my neck. She points to it and then meets my glare again. "Shit. You work here. I didn't know. I swear."

"And why should I believe you?"

"Because I have no reason to lie," Hayden says.

"Why are you here then?" I motion to the photograph I caught her gawking at earlier. "For the view?"

The tips of Hayden's ears pinken. She's embarrassed. *Well that's adorable. Wait. Stop. No.*

"My best friend brought me here," Hayden explains.

I overtly search the perimeter. "Your *imaginary* best friend?"

Hayden rolls her eyes. "Har. Har. No. I think she's in the dressing room."

I put my hands on my hips, about to call bullshit, but before I can get the words out, some perky blonde chick bounds in our direction and cheerfully wraps her arms around Hayden, who gives me a self-satisfied smirk. *Damn. Her friend is actually real. Now I look like a paranoid, narcissistic asshole. Great.*

"Hey!" Blondie says to Hayden. "I thought I lost you."

"Nope," Hayden says to her friend. "I've been right here."

Blondie grins at me. It's unsettling. "Aren't you going to introduce me to your friend?" She asks Hayden.

"Oh. We're not friends," I quickly say.

Blondie pouts and Hayden narrows those gorgeous blue eyes of hers at me. *Ah! Stop.*

"What are you talking about?" Hayden asks me exasperatedly. "We're totally friends!" She drapes her arm around Blondie's waist and gestures to me. "Ava, this is Blake. Blake, this is Ava."

Ava attempts to study me inconspicuously but much like Hayden, subtlety is not her strong suit.

"Blake from the bar Blake?" Ava asks Hayden.

I shoot Hayden a scornful look.

Hayden nods. "In the flesh."

I plaster on a smile and reach out my hand to Ava.

"Nice to meet you, Ava," I say.

Ava shakes my hand and smiles back. "Nice to meet you, too, Blake."

Hayden stares at my hand clasped within Ava's. *This is awkward.* I let go of Ava and point to the bra slung over her left shoulder.

"Those are buy one, get one free today," I say to Ava. "You can mix and match colors and styles."

Ava's eyes get bigger. "Really?"

I almost laugh. "Yup."

34

Ava unwraps herself from Hayden. "What would you recommend?" She asks me.

Hayden coughs and hits her chest with her fist. She glares at her best friend. "You can't ask her that."

I wave. "I'm right here and yes, she can ask me that. I'm the manager. It's my job to answer." I turn my attention to Ava, but I'm watching Hayden through the corner of my eye. "Well, I'm wearing the scoop demi bra. It has a more revealing neckline than the standard demi bra, but it's great for wearing with low-cut tops. It's lightly lined so it holds its shape and the underwire offers optimal support. It's super comfortable though. And it's one of our top-sellers. I'm a fan." I actually never tell customers what I wear. This is purely for Hayden's benefit. I point to Hayden's seemingly favorite picture in the store. "It's that one."

Ava crooks her neck to examine the bra depicted in the photograph. She grins and grabs Hayden's right arm. "What do you think?"

Hayden glances at the picture and then at me only her gaze lands on my chest and not my face. *Amateur.*

"Yeah. Hayden, what do you think?" I repeat Ava's question.
Hayden lowers her eyes to inspect her sneakers. "It's nice," she says quietly.

"I'm sold," Ava says to me. "But I'd want one that's more colorful."

Why am I not surprised? I smile at Ava. "You should check out the floral print collection by the perfume case near the registers."

"Awesome. Thank you," Ava says to me.

"You're welcome," I reply. "Let me know if you need any more help."

"I will." Ava pets Hayden's shoulder. "I'll be right back," she says and vanishes.

Hayden purses her lips, nods slowly and finally raises her eyes to meet mine. "Why do you take pleasure in messing with me?"

I shrug. "Not really sure...it's honestly almost too easy."

"I might've told Ava about you last night."

"Mhmm. That might've been implied," I retort.

"I swear I wasn't stalking you though." Hayden's expression suddenly twists into one of confusion. She glances in the general direction of where I told Ava to go and then looks at me almost apologetically.

"Whatever you say."

"Ava told me I could use more friends," Hayden says.

I silently groan. "And you're telling me this because...?"

"Have lunch with me tomorrow."

I let out a short laugh. "My god, woman. What is wrong with you? No."

Hayden stands up straighter. "I'm not trying to work a game on you."

"I should hope not because you clearly didn't practice after I told you to."

"I want to be your friend," Hayden says.

I sigh heavily. "Look, are you going to buy something or not? Because if not then I've got a job to do."

"I know. And I'll go, but just agree to have lunch with me tomorrow."

Aargh! "I'm working tomorrow. I can't."

Hayden inhales loudly through her nose. "Then have dinner with me tonight?"

Christ. She's relentless. "I'm closing tonight."

"Then it will be a late dinner," Hayden says.

"You'd like that, wouldn't you? To hang out with me late at night and make lame attempts to sweet talk me into

36

your bed."

Hayden scoffs. "If I didn't want to be your friend, I wouldn't ask you out to dinner or lunch or anything for that matter. I'd ask you to meet me when your shift is over, we'd fuck and then we'd part ways. The end."

Wow. I did not see that coming. Okay. I was wrong. The girl has game. I hold Hayden's stare for a moment then I graze my bottom lip with my top teeth and furnish an impish grin. "That wasn't half bad."

Hayden smiles. "Does that mean you'll have dinner with me to find out if we have a future as friends?"

I decide to grant Hayden's request if for no other reason than I neglected to grocery shop this week.

"I'm not going to sleep with you."

"What a relief," Hayden says.

I chuckle. "I get out at eleven."

Hayden grins. "What's your address? I'll pick you up."

"Haha. No. I'm not telling your stalker ass where I live. Have you lost your mind? You can meet me here in the plaza parking lot."

"Fine. Eleven o' clock. I'll be here." Hayden glimpses at the photograph behind her and then eyes me speculatively. "Is that really what you—"

"Don't."

"Right. It's not like I care anyway."

"Uh huh." I smirk and wave to Hayden. "Later," I say and walk towards the back office. It's not until I'm sitting at my desk that I become cognizant of the fact that I'm still smiling. *Fuck.*

Chapter Six

Hayden

"I cannot believe you did that to me!" I use my chopsticks to pick up and fling a carrot across the table at Ava. Ava dodges the flying vegetable. "Hey!" She chucks a piece of tofu at my head. *For two women in our thirties, we're incredibly sophisticated.*

I duck and the tofu lands on the floor by one of the legs of my chair. "Whoa! Watch the hat!"

Ava laughs. "Oh for crying out loud. Your precious hat is fine."

Ava and I are sitting in the mall food court dining on Pad Thai, surrounded by tables of tweens taking selfies or pictures of their food to post online. Most of the people taking their meals to go are wearing uniforms, name tags, or tee shirts with store logos on them. This particular section of the mall is unquestionably overrun with aromas. My nostrils are inundated by a variety of smells including but not limited to pizza, coffee, and fried dough. It's a miracle that my nose is able to perceive the food set right in front of me.

Once I'm sure that our mini food fight is over, I straighten myself in my seat and glare at my best friend. "I'm serious, Aves. How could you?"

"Technically I didn't do anything. I simply asked you to come to the plaza with me. That's all." Ava smiles and continues eating her noodles.

I press my lips into a thin line and shake my head. "Oh no you don't. You don't get to play innocent. You researched Blake online and found out that she works at Undercover and then you purposely brought me there without my even knowing that you were being shifty," I quietly fume. "I'm your best friend. You're not supposed to do duplicitous things to me. You trapped me."

Ava sighs. "I wasn't trying to deceive you. I was trying to help you."

"Help me with what? I didn't need help with anything."

"That's total bullshit. I'm certain I recall you droning on about how you enjoyed talking to her, and I thought it was ludicrous of you to not even want to make an attempt to find her. You clearly like her."

I feel the heat in my cheeks. "I told you already that I don't like her. Not like that."

"Ah. But you like her as a potential friend, and you *are* in dire need of a friend...one whom you don't live with. We covered this last night. Remember?"

I groan. "Yeah. I remember, but that doesn't make what you did right."

Ava shrugs. "Did you or did you not get a friend date out of this experience?"

I clench my jaw and squinch my eyes up at Ava. "I did," I say through gritted teeth.

Ava smirks. "Exactly."

"That still doesn't excuse your shiftiness."

Ava wipes her mouth with her napkin and clears her throat. *Here we go.* I mentally prepare for Ava's oncoming speech.

"Hayden, you made me promise not to tell you what I found out about her and I kept my promise," Ava says. "Yes. I discovered where she works but I honestly didn't know she'd be here today. I hoped that she would be, but it was total fate that she actually was there." Ava's face lights up. "Pretty effing cool, right?"

"Yeah. Right," I grumble.

"Listen, I love you and you wanted to be friends with someone but let's be real: you don't know how to make friends. You know how to charm women out of their clothes but making friends?" Ava winces. "Not your specialty."

I gape. "What? No. If memory serves, we became friends because of *me*. So there." I stick my tongue out at Ava.

"Ha! All you did was ask me which bed I wanted in our dorm room. And after I told you that you should get dibs since you got there before me and all, *I* invited *you* out for brunch and so began our friendship."

"I spoke first. I broke the ice."

Ava rolls her eyes and points one of her chopsticks at me. "Sorry, Ms. Walcott, you've been disqualified from this round. Next."

"Whatever."

"Whatever," Ava mimics my whiny tone. I break into a small smile. *Ugh. Why does she have to be so freaking cute?*

Ava takes a swig of her soda and swallows. "Dude, the bottom line here is that I saw an opportunity to lend you a hand in obtaining a friend and I took it because I care about you and voila! It worked. You're welcome."

I move the remaining noodles on my plate around with my chopsticks. "I appreciate your intentions but now she thinks I really am a stalker."

"Then tell her it was me."

"That'll sound even more pathetic." I chew on a piece of baby corn. "How did you even manage to find her with just a first name to go on?"

Ava grins. "I got mad skillz, homie."

I cringe. "Don't talk like that. It's weird."

Ava laughs. "Noted."

I wait but she doesn't say anything. "Well? How'd you do it? How'd you find her?"

"Do you really want to know?"

"Yes."

"Boston's not that big of a city. All I had to do was

narrow my Quest search to every Blake in and around town and there weren't many results so I went through each person's profile on Cyberjournal, looking for any possible social connection you two might have and I found one. Thus, I knew I had the right Blake. I then went to my source's profile page and was able to access Blake's profile page through them."

"Wow. Huh. So who's our mutual Cyberjournal friend?" I rack my brain. *Oh god. Is it someone we've both slept with?*

"Now that, I can't tell you."

"What? Why not?"

"Because I'd be breaking my promise to you about the information-giving and such," Ava says. "If you want to know who you're both connected to, you're gonna have to get to know her. Work it into the conversation…but casually. Or…" Ava smiles. "Maybe it will just come to you. Life is a funny thing, Hayden. A funny thing."

"I'm not laughing."

"That's because you're nervous."

I snort. "As if! Why would I even be nervous?"

"I don't know. You tell me," Ava says. "Maybe because you think she's attractive."

"I said she was alright. I never said she was attractive."

"Mhmm. Then look me in the eyes and tell me you didn't practically cum in your joggers when she was describing her bra. I mean, fuck. Even *I* was turned on."

My breath catches. "You were?"

"Yes. You weren't?"

"I…uh…this feels inappropriate. Can we talk about something else?" I ask. *Please.*

"Yeeeah." Ava drawls, nodding slowly. "You were turned on." She snickers and then continues talking about how much money she spent at Undercover and all I can think about is the idea of Ava getting turned on by Blake and how much *that* turns me on. My imagination begins to formulate a scenario involving the two of them in which they're...

"Hayden!" Ava snaps her fingers in front of my face

I blink. "What?"

"Where'd you go? You completely spaced out."

"I'm right here," I lie.

"Liar! You were just so distant. Off in your own head somewhere." Ava gasps. "You were thinking about Blake and the sexy bra. Weren't you?"

Something like that. "Psht. No I wasn't." I get up from my seat. "Can we finish up your retail therapy shit so that we can go home?"

Ava giggles. "You have guilty face," she says in a sing song manner and then mumbles, "Pervert."

I say nothing to dispute Ava's allegation. I just smirk. She's not entirely wrong.

Chapter Seven

Blake

It's only as I'm leaving Quincy Plaza after locking up Undercover for the night that I realize I have no idea *where* in the parking lot I'm supposed to be meeting Hayden. It's a fairly large parking lot. *Awesome.* Normally, in this sort of situation, I would call or text the person I have plans with but I don't have Hayden's number and she definitely doesn't have mine. *Obviously my being overly cautious has backfired. Fantastic.* As the mall doors close behind me, I barely have any time to problem solve this predicament, when I spot Hayden standing awkwardly by one of the large lamp posts lining the path from the plaza to the parking lot. She's not exactly leaning into the post but she's also not completely standing straight. Her shoulders are slightly hunched, one leg is crossed over the other so that her body weight is shifted more to the right, and her head is bent down a little. She's peering up at me from beneath the bill of her hat, smiling at me somewhat sheepishly. *Stop smiling at me and being all cute because I can't deal with it.*

As I continue walking towards her, I unwittingly cruise her. She's taller than me but not by much and I'm five feet and six inches tall. She's slender but not skeletal with an almost athletic build about her, but it's difficult to accurately assess her figure because of what she's wearing: semi-loose fitting sweatpants that are unmistakably men's though she pulls them off effortlessly, owning her style. A zip-up hoodie that hugs her body just enough to make me almost want to know what's beneath the sweatshirt. Almost.

Wait. Why did she opt not to change her outfit? Either she's being kind knowing that *I* didn't have the opportunity to change my clothes or she's trying to keep this get-together as casual and generic-like as possible, but for me, nothing about this feels even remotely ordinary. I don't meet up with women I hardly know to hang out with them; I meet up with women I hardly know to have sex with them and move on with my life afterwards. *Why did I put myself in this situation?* I'm silently scolding myself as I approach Hayden. Right when we are face to face, a light wind brushes by us and immediately Hayden's scent engulfs me. I lose my train of thought. *Where was I? Oh. Right. I don't want to do this.*

"Hi." Hayden offers me her signature smile, the confident one from when I first met her at the bar last night. I forget again that I don't want to be doing this. *Are all of her smiles so goddamned adorable?*

Another cool breeze snaps me back to reality. *Alright. Looks like we're doing this.* I smile back at Hayden. "Hey."

"How was work?" Hayden inquires.

"It was fine."

"Are you hungry?"

"I am, but it's late and most places are closed so I'm hoping you planned accordingly," I say.

Hayden grins. "How do you feel about pizza?"

I purse my lips thoughtfully. "I feel good about it."

"Cool. I know a spot." Hayden motions to the parking lot. "Are you okay with me driving?"

I narrow my eyes at Hayden. "Not really."

"Why? I'm an excellent driver."

I shrug. "You're also an excellent stalker and for all I know, an excellent kidnapper."

Hayden frowns. "I didn't stalk you. I can explain everything. And I won't kidnap you. I swear."

"I'm gonna take a gamble on you only because I'm starving."

"That's fair." Hayden reaches out her hand for me to take.

44

Is this a joke? Is she for real? I scoff at Hayden's outstretched hand. "I'm good. Thanks."

Hayden clears her throat. "Right. I was just…you know, to guide you to my car."

"To guide me? Right. Of course." I shake my head. "Thanks, but I'm totally capable of following you."

"Alright. Well, this way then." Hayden steps towards the parking lot and I plod alongside her until we reach a tan-colored station wagon. She unlocks the passenger side door and opens it for me. I give Hayden my side-eye, which is on point from twenty-nine years of living as a cynic.

"This isn't a date." I remind Hayden as I get inside the vehicle.

Hayden exhales heavily. "I know, but that doesn't mean I can't be courteous," she says as she rounds the car and slips into the driver's seat. She pats the console between our seats and looks at me. "What do you think?"

I glance around the inside of the station wagon and out the window. *What the fuck is she talking about?* I turn my attention to Hayden. "What do I think about what? I don't see anything."

"Leela, my car. What do you think of her?" Hayden grins boastfully.

Bahaha! Oh no. Hold up. Hayden's being serious. It takes all of my energy to suppress a laugh. I nod. "She's a real gem."

"You're being sarcastic?"

"I am."

"What don't you like about her?" Hayden asks.

"For fuck's sake, Hayden, just drive."

"No. Tell me what you think is wrong with her?"

I roll my eyes. "I don't think anything is wrong with her. Besides, even if I did, what would it matter? Nothing. Because it's–*she*–is your car so it only matters what you think." *Boom! Reverse psychology.*

"Ava hates her," Hayden says sullenly as she turns the engine. Once. Twice. Finally the car starts.

I shrug. "I'm sorry but how old are you?"

The car is in motion now, but as soon as Hayden stops at a red light, she squints over at me. "I'm thirty. Why?"

"No reason. I heard this ridiculous rumor once that by age thirty, no one should really give a shit what other people think."

Hayden smiles a little and looks ahead at the road in front of her. "I literally JUST turned thirty so technically I'm still kind of twenty-nine."

I chuckle. "Um. That's not how that works. If you just turned thirty then technically you're thirty."

Hayden raps her fingers against the steering wheel. "I suppose. And how old are you?"

"Twenty-nine."

"Are you worried about turning thirty?"

"No. Why? Were you?" I ask.

"Yes."

Part of me wants to question her more but I decide to hold off. I motion to the audio system in the car. "A cassette player, huh?"

"Yup." Hayden uses her right hand to open the console. "All of my mixed tapes are in here. You can put one in if you want."

"So to clarify: your mixed tapes are in the console of your station wagon?"

Hayden nods, smiling earnestly.

I bite back another laugh. "Wow. And here I was wondering why you had so much trouble picking up women."

Hayden reaches over and hits my outer left thigh playfully, but I'm too fast. I arrest her by the wrist before she can pull away. "Hands," I warn. I loosen my grip a bit and

Hayden wriggles free.

"My bad," Hayden says.

"It's okay but if it happens again, I break your arm."

Hayden chuckles. "Wow. And here *I* was wondering why *you're* still single."

I breathe out a small laugh. "Well…" I begin rummaging through Hayden's mix tape collection. "I choose to be single."

"Why's that?" Hayden asks. "Are you emotionally stunted? Did somebody hurt you?"

"No, I'm not emotionally stunted. Why the hell would you ask me that? Are you emotionally stunted?"

Hayden chews on her lower lip for a moment, drawing my attention to her lip ring. *And that full bottom lip.* "I might be. I mean I sleep around with women in some lame attempt to forget that I can't have the one woman I want." Unexpectedly, my gut twists and the air leaves my lungs. *Christ almighty.* I lift a tape from the console to disguise my discomposure. When my breath returns, I read the name of the tape aloud, "Hayden's Awesome Mix Volume One." I smirk and insert the tape. Seconds after hitting "play," an acoustic indie rock song begins thumping through the speakers. I quietly mouth the lyrics along with the lead singer.

Hayden eyes me again. "You like this song?"

"Who doesn't?"

"Lame people," she answers.

"Exactly." I pause for a second. "Does Ava like this song?" I watch the muscles in Hayden's jaw tense up.

"Not especially."

"Does that bug you?"

Hayden clears her throat. "No. Why would it?"

"No reason." I bob my head to the rhythm of the song a little more and then speak again. "You said you were going to explain to me about the stalking thing. So?"

Hayden slowly veers to the side of the street and parks alongside the curb in front what appears to be the smallest pizzeria I've ever seen. She shuts the car off and leans her head back. Instead of looking at me, Hayden closes her eyes and pinches the bridge of her nose with her left hand. She sighs.

"Last night, when I got home from Luscious, I told Ava about how I met you," Hayden says softly. "She's my roommate…and my bestie so we sorta tell each other everything. Anyways, Ava lectured me on how much I need more friends and thought I should pursue you as a friend, but I told her I didn't get your number; that I only knew your first name." Hayden winces. "Ava told me she'd find you on the internet because she was curious about who you were." Hayden shifts her gaze in my direction. "I maybe talked about you a lot…because of how standoffish you were and all."

I nod with an unamused smile. "Uh huh."

Hayden looks away from me. "I told her you didn't seem like you wanted me to pursue you in any kind of way and that she could do what she wanted with the knowledge of your first name. But, I made her promise not to tell me whatever she found out about you because if you wanted me to find out, you would have told me yourself." Hayden meets my eyes again. "Right? You would've told me?"

"Depends."

Hayden rubs the back of her neck. "Supposedly, we have a common friend on Cyberjournal and she went through their account to access yours."

Who do we both know? I think back to last night; to how Hayden had the bartender make me a gin and tonic. And to how the bartender seemed to know Hayden. The bartender. *Connor. We were both talking to Connor. Christ.*

Hayden grabs the steering wheel with both of her hands. "I didn't know that Ava discovered where you work. I woke up this morning and she asked me to go to the mall with her. I agreed. Once we got there, the first place she wanted to go was Undercover. I didn't realize—"

"That she was setting you up?"

The corners of Hayden's mouth turn down. "Yeah."

"Huh. So Ava's the real stalker and you're just...her sidekick?"

Hayden shakes her head. "Ava was just being silly and thought she could help me make a friend but neither of us had any way of knowing you'd be there today. So in some ways it *was* a coincidence."

"Don't push it."

"Sorry."

"Alright. Well, I appreciate your explanation." I unfasten my seatbelt. "Can we eat now?"

Hayden stares at me quizzically. I simply stare back.

"Okay," Hayden says. "Yeah. We can eat. Of course."

Hayden and I both get out of the car and look at one another from across the low roof of the station wagon.

"One more thing," I say.

"What's that?"

"Did Ava tell you who our mutual contact is?"

"No because of the promise she made not to tell me anything she found out," Hayden says.

"You're not curious? Not even a teensy bit?"

Hayden gapes. "Why? Do you know?"

"Of course I do."

"How?"

I smirk. "I pay attention."

"Okay. Who is it then?"

"I thought you didn't want to know," I say.

"I changed my mind. I want to know."

"Connor Tamblyn."

"What?! Connor? How do you figure?" Hayden

stammers.

"I know Connor and I saw him talking to you at the bar. He might've given me the vague impression that you two knew each other. And you *did* confirm that you were a regular at Luscious. He has to be our common denominator."

Hayden grins. "You saw Connor talking to me?"

I shrug. "Yeah. And?"

"So you were watching me?"

I roll my eyes. "Don't."

Chapter Eight

Hayden

While Blake browses through the few pages that make up the menu at Sebastian's Brick Oven Pizzeria, or "Bastian's" as I like to call it for simplicity purposes, I take her in. Even though a table is set between us, it's a small table and she feels awfully close. Despite the strong aromas of garlic and onion that saturate the air around us, I can smell her. She smells of lilacs after a spring rainfall; the kind of smell you breathe in with your eyes closed.

Blake hasn't altered her appearance in any way since I saw her earlier at Undercover, but for some reason in the very poor lighting of Bastian's, she's even more appealing. *How is that possible?* Similar to last night, Blake's wearing mascara and lightly tinted lip gloss, which I'm going to guess are her staples when it comes to makeup. Her brown hair is down again but some type of product is making it look more curly than wavy at the ends. She's dressed in dark blue skinny jeans that are designedly ripped at the knees, a black ruffle-trim long sleeved babydoll top, and matching black flats. My eyes betray me and roam over her top once more. I try with all of my might to not envision what's beneath her shirt. *Don't think about the picture. Don't think about the picture.* And without a moment's notice, I'm imagining Blake's lacy bra.

Blake peers at me from the top of her menu. "Are you done yet?" Blake asks.

There is no way she caught me checking her out. I widen my eyes and raise my brows to appear to be perplexed.

"I'm sorry? Done with what?" I respond.

The left corner of Blake's mouth quirks up into a half-smirk. "Sizing me up."

Fuck. "Psht. Nooo. That's not...I wasn't...I was just...I

51

like your nose ring." *Oh because that was smooth. Way to go, champ.*

Blake purses her shiny lips together. "Oh. Okay," she says dubiously. "Well, thank you."

"You're welcome." I take a sip of my water. "Do you know what you're going to order?"

Blake shuts her menu and places it on the table. "Wanna split a plain cheese pizza with me?"

"Sounds good." I flag down the only waiter in the joint by waving my napkin in the air. As he starts towards our table, I glance at Blake. "Um. Did you want a drink?"

"A drink would be great." Blake smiles at me.

I nod. "Right. So since gin and tonic isn't your drink, this would probably be the best time for you to tell me what exactly your drink is."

"What's *your* drink?"

I chuckle. "I asked you first."

"I asked you second and since you're taking me out to try to be my friend, I think you should give me this one."

I press my tongue against my bottom teeth. *Unbelievable.* "Fine. Vodka tonic."

Blake squints at me. "Interesting. I wouldn't have guessed that."

"Too stereotypically hetero?"

Blake laughs. "Little bit."

I shrug. "I'm a puzzle to be solved." I motion to her. "And for you?"

"Beer. Porter," Blake says. "The darker, the better."

I open my mouth but close it quickly. "Alright."

"Too stereotypically dyke-ish?" There's amusement in Blake's question.

I bite back a laugh of my own. "You said it."

"Hi. Welcome to Sebastian's Pizzeria. I'm Zack," a boy of no more than twenty-two years old says to me and Blake.

"I'll be your waiter." He smiles. "What can I get for you two?"

I clear my throat. "Hi, Zack. We'll have a large cheese pizza and two glasses of whatever porter you have on tap. Please."

Zack jots this information down on his notepad and nods. "Will that be all?"

"Yes," I say.

"Sure." Zack takes our menus off the table. "It'll be about fifteen minutes," he says and walks away.

Blake frowns at me. "You don't always have to drink the same thing as me."

"I know that. I wanted beer...it pairs well with pizza," I explain. "Besides, the mixed drinks here are mediocre at best."

"Alright. Fair enough." Blake searches the area. "So how did you find this place?"

"College," I say. "I used to order take-out from here at least once a week while I was up all hours of the night writing papers and whathaveyou."

"College," Blake repeats slowly. "Where did you go to school?"

I sigh. "Miranda University."

"That's cool. I've heard good things about MU. What did you study?"

"Lesbianism." I smirk.

Blake chuckles. "I'm guessing you graduated at the top of your class then?"

My smirk turns into a smile. "Does it bother you that I don't pass as straight?"

Blake's warm brown eyes suddenly blacken. "Excuse me? Do you seriously think I'm that much of an asshole? I don't care what the fuck you look like or how you present yourself. Why? Does it bother you that I *do* pass?" She's practically seething.

I hold up my palms. "Whoa, whoa, whoa. I obviously struck a nerve and I apologize," I say. "I don't think you're an asshole and no. It doesn't bother me that you pass." I wrap both of my hands around my glass of water. "It's a little intimidating…like how pretty you are, but that's…" *No! Stop talking! Oh my god, stop talking!* I wince. "Sorry. I don't even know why I said that."

Blake's shoulder muscles relax as she studies my expression. "It's okay. I appreciate the compliment."

"I majored in Advertising," I say to steer our conversation back on course.

"Oh. So what do you do for work?"

I groan. "Not advertising."

"Wow. Sounds fascinating," Blake says.

I exhale. "I'm an administrative assistant at Rose Family Auto downtown."

Blake nods. "Do you like it? You made it seem as though you were disappointed that you weren't in advertising what with the dramatic groan and all."

"It pays the bills." I lean back in my seat. "Did you go to college?"

Blake crinkles her nose. "Nah. It wasn't for me."

"But you enjoy your job?"

"I do." Blake nods. "It's demanding and sometimes the schedule sucks, but I do well for myself."

"Here you are," Zack says as he places the pizza in the center of the table.

"Thanks," Blake and I say simultaneously.

"You're welcome." Zack takes two glasses of beer off his serving tray and sets them on the table by our food. "Anything else?"

"We're good for now," I say.

Zack gives us a thumbs up and vanishes again.

I motion to the pizza. "You can pick the first slice."

Blake rolls her eyes. "Awe. How generous. I am going to take the biggest slice just so you know."

"Go for it."

Blake disregards the spatula and uses her hands to transfer a slice of pizza from the platter onto her plate. I'm not sure why but it makes me smile. I raise my glass of beer.

"Cheers," I say.

"Really?"

"Yes. Really."

"Ugh." Blake holds up her glass. "Alright. On with it."

I stick my tongue out at her. "Cheers to our newly forming friendship."

"That was so corny," Blake says and clinks her glass against mine. "Cheers." She takes a long drink and then starts eating. "Holy fuck! This is good pizza."

I laugh. "It's very unladylike to talk with food in your mouth."

Blake swallows and sticks her tongue out at me. "Do you come here with Ava?"

I nearly choke on the pizza in my mouth. I hold up a finger, signaling for Blake to give me a second. I take a sip of my beer and cough. "Sorry. It went down the wrong way."

"Mhmm."

"Um. No," I say. "I've only ever come here alone but we've had it together. At the dorm. At home. Why?"

Blake shakes her head. "Just asking."

There's a small smile playing on Blake's lips that's freaking me out. "What?"

"What what?"

"What is that look you're giving me?" I ask.

Blake wipes her mouth with her napkin. "It's Ava, isn't it?"

My heart violently plummets into my stomach. "Is what Ava?"

"Is Ava the woman you were referring to earlier? The one you want but can't have? The reason for your...promiscuity?"

She sure is. "Psht."

Blake snickers and takes another bite of pizza. "She straight?"

I chew my own food slowly to avoid the rest of this conversation for as long as I can. After I swallow, I take a drink. Finally, I look over at Blake, who's staring at me expectantly.

"Yes," I say. "Ava's straight."

Blake sucks in a breath. "Yeah. She's right. You *do* need friends."

"Thanks," I say dryly.

"Does she know how you feel?"

"No. That's never...no."

"But you think sleeping with other women is going to help you get over her?" Blake asks.

"Not at all, but it helps me forget."

"Does it though?"

Not one bit. "Sorta."

Blake licks the tomato sauce off of her pinky and the sight of her tongue causes my heart to trip.

"Relax," Blake says. "I'm not going to judge you."

"It's fucked up. I know."

Blake inhales through her nose. "Everyone's fucked up a little."

"Are you admitting that you're fucked up a little too then?"

"Definitely." Blake grins, but her features quickly become somber. "Listen. You sleep around to escape. I sleep around because I love women and I love sex," Blake informs me. "And because I'm choosing to never ever put myself in a situation where someone could hurt me again. Ever." She swallows a mouthful of beer. "You asked me in the car if someone had hurt me. There it is. The answer is yes. Someone hurt me." Blake wags her finger. "But never again."

"Do you want to talk about it?"

"Nope. I do not." Blake finishes off her second slice of pizza. "Do you want to talk about how in love you are with your best friend who is also your roommate?"

My gut wrenches. "I never said I was in love with her."

"True, but you're an easy read. Remember?"

"Right." I tear apart a piece of crust. "So, how do you know Connor?"

Blake glances thoughtfully at the ceiling of Bastian's and then her gaze meets mine. There are golden rays in the irises of her medium brown eyes that I hadn't noticed before now and for a split second I slip up and surrender to her breathtaking beauty. For a split second, I lose myself in her eyes.

"Connor and I go way back," Blake says.

"How far back?"

"We dated for like a second in high school."

I gasp. "Wow. For real?"

"Yup. One whole month."

I nod. "What happened?"

"You're very nosy."

"I know."

Blake shakes her head but smiles. "His penis happened."

I scrunch up my face. "Ew! Gross!"

Blake chuckles. "Hey. You asked." She nods. "Yeah. Dude took my virginity and it was during those two minutes that I realized I was totally gay."

I cover my mouth with my hand to muffle my laugh.

"We're still friends though," Blake adds. "Connor's a

good guy." She smiles at me conspiratorially. "Don't tell him I told you."

I smile back. "I won't." I point to her empty glass. "Do you want another beer?"

"No. I'm all set. We should head back soon though. It's late."

"You don't want dessert or anything?" I ask.

"My goodness, woman. You *are* obsessed with me. Always trying to prolong our time together and shit."

Instantly, my face and my ears are ablaze. "No. No. No. I was just—"

"I'm teasing. Don't be embarrassed." Blake smirks and before I can protest or even take my next breath, she's reaching across the table with both of her arms. My heart comes to a complete stop. Blake grabs onto my ears and squeezes them. "These suckers here are your biggest tell."

I pout. "I know."

We stare at each other in silence for a fraction of minute and that's all the time it takes for me to envision Blake in her lacy underthings...and nothing else. *Oh boy.*

Chapter Nine

Blake

It occurs to me that I've been cupping Hayden's ears in my hands a second too long when her pale blue eyes become especially bright and I feel her jaw flex beneath my wrists...and the slightest urge to pull her closer rushes through me. Hastily, I release her, silently steel myself, and airily return to my seat. *What are you doing, you fucking idiot? Why did you touch her? What the hell was that? Okay. Be cool.* I regard Hayden with pursed lips.

"Your ear-blushy thing...It's endearing," I say with as much indifference as I can muster. *Oh. No. Uh-uh. Your ear-blushy thing? No. Alright, you're done.*

Hayden smiles shyly. "Thanks a bunch."

I laugh lightly. "No prob. So I really should be heading home. I have work in the morning. Adulting and all that jazz."

"I understand." Hayden slides out of her seat. "I'll pay at the counter on the way out. Do you want to wait here or...?"

"Yeah. I'll stay here." I watch Hayden until she's out of view and then I pull my phone out of jeans pocket. I swipe on the Scrolling Singles dating app. For several minutes, my finger hovers over my inbox, where there are three new unread messages awaiting me.

"Scrolling Singles, huh?" Hayden's voice startles me from behind. "Do you really need to get home to rest up for work or are you looking to get laid after this?"

I smirk. "Not that it's any of your business, but I do have sleep to catch up on."

Hayden raises an eyebrow at me. "I don't believe you."

"Believe what you want. I don't give a shit."

Hayden nods. "Okay then. Well, the bill's paid." She motions towards the exit of Sebastian's Pizzeria. "Ready?"

"Ready."

The first half of our fifteen-mile drive back to the plaza's parking lot is loaded with silence. I stare out the window and listen to Hayden's thumbs tap against the steering wheel in time with the music playing from the radio.

I turn to look at Hayden. "Do you ever think about telling Ava how you feel about her?" I internally roll my eyes at my own question.

Hayden's grip on the wheel tightens. "No."

"Isn't that...I don't know...painful?"

Hayden shrugs. "I've had feelings for her since I was eighteen. I'm thirty now. Throughout the years, I've mastered suppressing all those emotions."

"Right. By sleeping around?"

Hayden glances over at me. "Yes. Why do you ask?"

"Well, as your potential friend, if you want to talk about it ever..."

"I don't," Hayden says. "Thanks though."

"Sure."

"Do I get to ask you a hard question now?"

Ugh. I totally set myself up for this. "Go ahead."

"Why am I not your type?"

Jesus. "It has nothing to do with your outward appearance if that's what you're worried about."

"I'm not worried. I'm just curious." Hayden suddenly grins at me. "I mean you did confess to watching me at the bar. Do you usually check out women who aren't your type?"

"Actually, I was checking you out as a prospect for my friend, Grace." *This is one hundred percent untrue.*

60

"While she was hooking up with someone in the bathroom?" Hayden probes.

"Yup."

"Wow. You're a thorough wing woman."

"I do my best."

"So I'm guessing I wasn't her type either?" Hayden asks.

"Not necessarily but her stint in the bathroom went over well so that was that."

"Makes sense. I get it." Hayden nods. "You know, if you have a type and you want to tell me being that we're friends and stuff, that'd be cool."

I scoff. "Oh. So we're *officially* friends now, is that it?"

"It is."

"That escalated quickly."

Hayden just smiles and continues driving. After we go a few more miles, we reach the Quincy Plaza. When Hayden pulls into near-vacant mall parking lot, I point to my black sedan. "Over there. That's me."

Hayden slows her station wagon as we near my car. She cuts the engine once her vehicle is next to mine. She looks out the window past me and examines my sedan.

"Nice ride," Hayden says.

"So I've been told." I wink at her.

Hayden pouts. "What is it with you and teasing me?"

"I told you, it's easy and besides, that's what friends do." I grin.

"Ha!" Hayden points at me. "So you DO agree that we're officially friends?"

"Don't jizz yourself just yet. I'm still feeling you out."

"Alright. Well, can I friend request you on Cyberjournal?"

"No and I'd appreciate it if both you and your bff refrain from stalking me online."

"We can do that."

I arch an eyebrow at Hayden. "Mhmm. We'll see."

"Do we at least get to exchange phone numbers?"

"Can you not blow up my phone if we do?"

"Yes."

I hold out my hand. "Give me your phone."

Hayden's forehead wrinkles. "Why?"

"Do you or do you not want my digits?" I ask.

Hayden eyes my open palm for a moment then reaches in her pants pocket, retrieves her cellphone and places it in my hand. I quickly program my contact information into Hayden's phone and give it back to her.

"All set," I say.

Hayden shoves her phone back inside her pocket. "You're difficult."

"Then why do you want to be my friend?"

Hayden runs her hand over her face and sighs. Then she fixes her eyes on me. "You intrigue me."

I take Hayden's admission as a compliment. I purse my lips. "Okay." I reach up and latch onto the bill of her hat. I tilt it to the side a little. "There." I snicker.

"Hey!" Hayden objects and lifts her hand to readjust her hat, but I lightly bat her arm away.

"Leave it," I say. "Please."

Hayden glares at me and frowns. There's something about the look she's giving me. *Damnit.* I feel a twinge of my own sadness begin to surface. *Just tell her.* I blow out a long breath as I unfasten my seatbelt. Then I shift in the passenger's side so that I'm facing Hayden.

"You remind me of her," I say softly.

"Who?"

"Sarah. My ex."

Hayden opens her mouth but snaps it shut quickly. "The one who hurt you?"

I press my lips together in a forced smile. "That's the only ex I have so yeah. That one."

Hayden nods. "Is that why I'm not your type?"

"Yahtzee."

"Do you want to talk about it?"

"I just did."

"Do you want to talk about it more?" Hayden asks.

"Nope."

Suddenly Hayden's hand is on my knee and we lock eyes. My heart stutters, betraying me. I go to swallow but my throat's locked.

"I'm not her," Hayden whispers. "I won't hurt you."

Ah yes. The most bullshit lie spoken by anyone ever.

I find my breath and gently swat her touch away. "I know you won't because I'll never give you the opportunity to."

"But even if you did—"

"I won't," I blurt.

"That's fine, but regardless, I won't hurt you. I don't hurt my friends."

"It's not about you," I say. "People hurt each other. It's what we do."

"Not always." A small lopsided smile spreads across Hayden's lips. "Stop being so cynical."

"I'm a realist. We've been through this already."

"Well then stop being such a realist." Hayden's still speaking softly.

"Why don't you stop being such an optimist?"

"Visionary." Hayden's pale blue eyes search mine intently. "I'm a visionary," she repeats quietly.

"Is that right?"

"That's right."

"Well, Visionary One, it's getting late. I need my beauty rest." I flip my hair jokingly but mostly I do it as an excuse to back away from Hayden a little. Our faces were a bit too close there.

Hayden chuckles half-heartedly. "I still don't believe that you're going straight to bed after this."

"I still don't give a shit what you believe." I smirk.

Hayden nods. "Right. So, um…I'll text you soon and perhaps we could hang out again?"

I raise my eyebrows at Hayden. "Yes. Perhaps." I turn and open the passenger side door. "Thanks for dinner," I say as I lift myself out of the station wagon.

"You're welcome."

As I close the door to the station wagon and start walking towards my own car, I hear Hayden call after me. Her voice is muffled but I can make out with perfect clarity what she says: "Goodnight, Blake."

I'm silently grateful that Hayden can't see me smiling like a schoolgirl because I'm horrified about the lack of control I have over my facial expression. More than that, I'm horrified at what my facial expression even is! I keep walking, feigning obliviousness, but as I do so, I raise my hand up in a mock wave. "Goodnight, Hayden," I mouth.

Chapter Ten

Hayden

I carefully balance a steaming cup of coffee in my left hand while using my right hand to manipulate the cursor on my laptop so that I can scroll through my newsfeed on Cyberjournal. I've only been awake for forty-five minutes this Sunday morning and I've already looked at Blake's profile page three times, chickening out on sending her a friend request each time. I know she told me not to and I'm not sure why I'm struggling so hard to respect that, but I am. The struggle is real.

"Good morning," Ava says through a yawn as she strides past me at the table and towards the coffee maker.

"Good morning." I watch Ava pour coffee and cream into a large mug, but really what I'm watching more than anything else is how the short shorts she sleeps in creep up in the back enough for me to see almost the entirety of her ass cheeks. I smirk to myself.

Once Ava's done fixing her cup of coffee, she turns and comes back in my direction. She slides into the seat across from me at the kitchen table. "I'm guessing you got home way late last night since I went to bed at one in the morning and your butt still wasn't here."

I nudge my laptop a little bit to the left to get a clearer view of Ava. I give her a small smile. "Yeah. It was pretty late."

Ava grins. "Did you guys sleep together?"

I gape. "No! Why would you say that?"

Ava chuckles. "Um. Because I know you. Duh." She shrugs. "Also that chick is a looker...and that bra. Man oh man."

I laugh. "Are you sure *you* don't want to sleep with her?"

"Positive." Ava takes a careful sip of her coffee. "Did she like Sebastian's?"

"She said she did."

"Are you going to hang out with her again?" Ava asks.

I swill the last bit of lukewarm coffee around the bottom of my mug and then swallow it back. "I think so. I mean, we're kind of friends now so it would make sense to hang out. You know?"

"Totes." Ava motions to my computer. "Did you find her online?"

"Possibly."

"Yeah. You did." Ava laughs. "Are you going to friend request her?"

I shrug. "I thought about it but I remain undecided."

"Just do it."

"No. It requires more consideration," I say *And Blake's permission*. "Anywho, I happened to see Blake on her Scrolling Singles app and I'm thinking that's the way you should go."

Ava scrunches up her face in disgust. "Ugh. I don't want to meet people in such an impersonal way."

"C'mon. We talked about you trying."

Ava rolls her eyes. "I know. I know."

I smile. "Maybe we could sign you up and create your profile?"

"Maybe you could make me an omelet and we can discuss this cyber dating business over breakfast?"

I sigh. "If I cook, do you promise you'll let me sign you up?"

Ava half-closes her eyes and hangs her tongue out of the side of her mouth in resistance. I have to laugh at how ridiculous she appears.

"No answer. No food," I say.

Ava pouts. "Aargh. Fine. If you feed me, I'll sign up but I have a condition."

I arch an eyebrow. "Oh? What's your condition?"

"I get to quit whenever I so please."

I purse my lips. "Hmm. No." I shake my head. "You have to at least give it two weeks and then you can quit whenever you'd like."

"One week," Ava counters.

"Ten days."

Ava sets down her mug and runs her finger along its rim thoughtfully. After a few seconds, she looks at me and holds out her hand for me to shake. "Deal."

I take her hand in mine. *How is her skin always so fucking soft?* "Alright. I'll get to cooking then."

Ava is still chewing the final bite of her omelet as she points to the screen of my laptop, where the first page of her Scrolling Singles profile is displayed, and says, "This is so lame."

I finish my second cup of coffee, swallow and shake my head. "Come on! It's not lame. Everybody does it."

"You don't do it."

True. "Okay. No, I don't. But, I've thought about it and besides, Blake does it and she thinks it's the best way to go. That said, let us continue." I move the cursor on my computer to the next section of the profile, where the user clicks on the sexuality they identify with. I scroll until I see the word 'straight' but before I can choose it, Ave grabs my wrist. I go still.

"Wait," Ava says. "Can we talk about something?"

I raise an eyebrow at her. "Are you deflecting?"

"No."

I sigh. "What's up?"

Ava frowns and looks away from me. "I don't know my sexuality….I don't think."

I forget to breathe for a second. *What is she talking about? Am I dreaming? I've definitely had a fantasy that starts off something like this.* I swallow. "What do you mean?"

Ava shrugs one shoulder. "You're going to think I'm crazy."

"I won't. I would never think that. You're my best friend. This is a safe space." *Please be into girls.*

"Okay." Ava exhales. "Something strange happened yesterday when we were in Undercover."

My gut twists immediately. *No! Does she have a crush on Blake?* I do my best to stay composed and nod. "Alright. What happened?"

Ava slowly raises her eyes to mine. *God. She's beautiful.*

"When I saw that picture...the one Blake pointed out to us...with the bra," Ava sputters. "I got excited." Ava lowers her gaze again. "Like sexually."

Whenever Ava confides in me that something turns her on, it takes all of my self-control to keep my thoughts clean and ignore my own arousal.

I offer another nod. "Okay. It was a sexy picture. You're human. That's a totally normal reaction. No big."

Ava presses her lips together tightly and winces. "That's not all."

My chest hurts. "What else is there?"

"I spent all last night thinking about how that picture made me feel and I realized that it's not the first time I found myself turned on by a woman," Ava says quietly.

I want to ask her what other women has she been turned on by. I want to ask her if she's ever been turned on by me. Instead I ask, "What are you saying?"

"I'm not entirely sure. Um. I guess...like maybe I'm not completely straight?"

Shit. This is really happening. In my fantasies, this is

the part where I kiss Ava but that would be highly inappropriate to do right now considering this is real life. "Do you think that you're…" I pause. *What do I say?* I clear my throat. "Do you think that you're…I don't know…gay?"

Ava blows out a breath as she tosses her head back. After a few seconds of silence, she looks at me. "I don't think so but I'm not certain either. It's like throughout my whole life no guy has ever really done it for me. And I kept thinking I just haven't met the right guy yet because that's pretty much what society tells you to think before you come to any conclusion that maybe it's because you're queer. You know? But it doesn't matter. Even with celebrities. I can see that guys are attractive but they don't turn me on. Not the way that picture at Undercover did." Ava shuts her eyes. "Not the way women do." She opens her eyes. They're filled with tears. "All this time what if my dating life has sucked so bad because I was dating guys when I should've been dating women?" She sniffles. "I've tried so hard for so long to convince myself this was all a phase and that eventually, I'd meet some amazing guy and that would be that, but I don't think that's what this is and last night was the first time I ever really allowed myself to question my sexuality and now I'm fucking terrified. Aargh!" Ava presses her palm against her forehead. "Or what if I'm wrong still? What if I'm bisexual? How do I not know what I am? Why is this so goddamned confusing?"

Her last word comes out as a sob. I inch my chair closer to Ava's and wrap my arms around her. Even unshowered, the woman smells fantastic.

"It's okay." I speak softly and rub her back. "You're okay."

After a few minutes, Ava's sniveling subsides and she easily unravels herself from my embrace. She wipes her nose on the back of her left hand and takes a deep breath.

"Sorry. I didn't mean to have a mental breakdown," Ava says through a soft laugh.

I smile. "Totally fine."

"Do you think I'm crazy?"

"Not at all."

Ava shakes her head. "Is this common? For a person to turn thirty-one and suddenly have an identity crisis?"

I chuckle. "You're not having an identity crisis, Aves. And people question who they are in all kinds of ways at all different ages: their sexuality, their purpose in the world, their passions, their assigned gender, their careers, and so on. It's part of what makes life so complicated but also so amazing."

Ava motions to the Scrolling Singles profile page that's open on my laptop. "What now?"

"I'm not sure I understand what you're asking?"

"Well, I think it's safe to say I'm not heterosexual but I don't know what label feels right for me. Do I have to have a label? Ugh. I hate this."

"You absolutely don't need a label. I think society prefers that you *do* have a label for the sake of making things easier to understand, but that's your choice. However, when it comes to dating site profiles, it's a little helpful for everyone if you have a label. You don't have to marry the label and you can change it whenever you want." I touch the screen of my computer. "How about bi-curious or heteroflexible or questioning?"

Ava's eyes widen. "'Questioning' is an option?"

"Totally."

For the first time since her confession, she smiles. "That's me! I'm questioning."

I hold my balled up fist to Ava and she bumps it with her own.

"Rock on!" I holler and Ava grins. "Now it's only a

matter of time until you realize that you're in love with me," I joke. Except for the fact that I'm not joking at all. I'm secretly divulging a wish.

Ava giggles and hits my arm. "You wish," she says as if she had just read my mind.

If you only knew. I playfully wink and turn my attention to Ava's online dating profile. I resume filling it out, all the while thinking that she is right...I do need a friend other than her.

Chapter Eleven

Blake

When Kendall comes back from her lunch break, I decide the store can function in my absence for a few minutes so that I can pee. After reminding myself multiple times that my assistant manager is competent and my staff is solid, I feel less guilty about leaving and rush to the bathroom.

While on the toilet, I pull my phone out from where I've been hiding it in my bra. Normally, I follow the same store policies that I enforce such as leaving one's cellphone in one's locker. However, I thought for sure that I'd wake up this morning to a missed call or text from Hayden only I didn't. Now I'm obsessively wondering why. *Did she not like me the way I thought she did? Why does it even matter? I didn't call or text her. It doesn't matter. I don't care one way or the other. I really don't care.* I swipe over my phone's screen to check for any notifications or voice messages. Nothing. *What the hell?!*

I wince. *Aaand so much for not caring.* "What is your issue?" I whisper to myself.

I glance at the time at the top corner of the screen. I elect to spend no more than five minutes on Cyberjournal to see what's going on. That is lie. I'm actually going to see if I can hunt down Hayden's profile. It takes me all of two minutes to track her down. Due to the fact that we are not official Cyberjournal friends, I'm limited to the amount of information and pictures I can access on her profile page. I stare at the "friend request" button for a few seconds then shake my head and silently ream myself out for even considering asking her to be my friend online. That would for one thing be uber hypocritical since I told her specifically NOT to friend request me. Also, it would make me look wicked desperate. I don't need her as a Cyberjournal friend. Hell, in all actuality, I don't even need her as a regular friend. Okay. It's settled. No online friend requests shall be sent. I exhale, satisfied with my sensible decision. I look away from her profile picture and try to pretend as though I didn't just notice what a good angle the photograph was taken from. My decision from a millisecond ago waivers. *My god! Stop!* I tap my phone against my forehead repeatedly to beat the temporary insanity from myself. I hear a beep. I freeze. I listen quietly. I'm definitely the only person in the bathroom. That beep definitely came from my phone. And it wasn't just any old beep, it was the sound that lets you know you've successfully sent a friend request to someone on Cyberjournal. I squeeze my eyes shut and swallow. I slowly move my phone away from my head and into my line of sight. I stare at the screen. Yup. I totally just friend requested Hayden. *Fuck me.*

I take a deep breath to keep myself from throwing my phone against the door of the bathroom stall. I turn off the heinous device and return it to its hiding spot in my bra. I get off the toilet seat, pull my jeans up, tuck in my blouse and use my foot to flush. I press my hands into the sides of the stall to steady myself. I take a second deep breath. I can't believe that just happened. Now what the fuck do I do if she doesn't accept my friend request? I'll be the world's biggest dipshit. I can't allow that. *I need a plan. What's my damage control plan?* The problem-solving part of my brain completely bails on me. *Think!*

Before I can form a thought, the bathroom door opens and I snap back to reality. *Work. I have to be at work.* I quickly exit the stall and hurry back to the sales floor.

"Where should these go?" Julie's staring at me, holding an armful of our new line of women's boxer briefs. It's almost five o' clock and the store's traffic has finally slowed down. Sunday is the only day we close early, which means we'll be closing in about an hour. *I cannot wait to be home.*

I point to a circular display table by the front of the store. "Right over there."

Julie nods. "Got it."

"I'll help you," I say and walk to the other side of the store with Julie. I need the distraction.

Julie and I begin arranging the new inventory. For a half of a second, my mind forsakes me and I imagine Hayden wearing a pair of the boxer briefs. I clear my throat and continue organizing the display.

"You okay?" Julie asks me.

I look up at my co-worker. "Yeah. Yeah. All good."

Julie holds up a pair of the briefs. "I really like these. I think they'll sell well."

I force a smile. "That's the goal."

Julie folds the pair in her hands and carefully places them on the table. "Would you wear them?" She asks without meeting my eyes.

Every so often, Julie and Kendall will ask me something that somehow alludes to lesbianism and because they're always terrified of offending me, their mostly stereotypical questions genuinely amuse me. I smile to myself as I pick up another pair to fold.

"Not my style," I say. "Would you?"

Julie purses her lips. "Nah. I couldn't rock them. Not my style either. I can definitely picture them on different girls though." There's a pregnant pause. "Who was that woman you were talking to in here yesterday?"

My chest tightens. *Christ almighty.* I glance over at Julie. "Who?" Of course I know she's referring to Hayden, but she doesn't have to know that I know that.

"The cute one with the hat."

I pretend to rack my brain. "Oh. Her. She's just a friend."

Julie tries to hide a small smile. "Huh."

I stop what I'm doing and raise an eyebrow at Julie. "What?"

Julie shakes her head. "Nothing." She steps back from the table and nods approvingly at her handiwork. "She could rock these. Your friend."

I cough on the air in the room. *Yeah she could.* I shrug. "I suppose," I say. "I hadn't really thought about it." *Lie.*

"You should tell her about them. It might help boost sales." There's a hint of playfulness in Julie's voice.

I narrow my glare at Julie. "Are you being smart with me?"

Julie gasps out a small laugh. "What? No."

My section of the table is organized exactly how it needs to be and honestly, so is Julie's, but I point to her side of the display anyway. "Can you please fold that pile so it lies more flat." It's not a question. It's an order.

Julie frowns. She knows I'm being a bitch to spite her. "They're as flat as they're going to—"

"Thanks," I say and head back to the register.

I still haven't left the mall parking lot. I'm sitting inside of my car with the heat turned on low. It's chilly on this particular September night. I'm trying to psyche myself up for hitting the grocery store on the way home. I think about crowded aisles and long lines and promptly decide that I can survive one more night having cereal for dinner.

I turn the keys in the ignition, but keep the car in park, not quite ready to leave because I'm not quite ready to deal with my Cyberjournal faux pas from earlier today. I try to recall the contents in my liquor cabinet. I settle on the bottle of Shiraz I know is there. *Okay. Now I'm ready.* I take my phone out of my pocket and turn it on. Instantly, it beeps several times to alert me of the messages I have: six texts from Grace, four notifications from Tap That, and two from Scrolling Singles, one missed call from an unknown number, and a voice message. Nothing from Cyberjournal. *Seriously? She couldn't even accept my friend request? It was her fucking idea in the first place. What the fuck?* I groan and log into my voicemail. I play the message.

My heartbeat times out at the sound of Hayden's voice. "Hey, Blake. It's me, Hayden. I was thinking...well I wanted to know...er...I guess I just thought we could talk. You know...because we're friends and stuff. Um. Yeah. So this is my number. Call me back...if you want. Only call me back if you want. Okay. Bye."

I listen to the message again. I smile at the way Hayden says my name and then smack my palm against the side of my head for smiling. I begin to wonder why she ignored me on social media but opted to call me, which is far more personal. I listen to the message again and vow not to smile. I succeed. Something about Hayden's tone sounds off. *Is she upset? Why would she be upset? Whoa. Why am I caring?* "Aargh!"

I shift gears, ease my right foot onto the gas pedal, and start driving. I resolve to not be angry with Hayden for neglecting my friend request and making me feel like a loser because maybe something is wrong and she really does need to talk. Maybe she does need a friend. Maybe I should attempt to be a real friend to her. *Fucking A.* I'll call her when I get home...post alcohol consumption...because is this even my life?

Chapter Twelve

Hayden

I'm in my room sitting cross-legged on my bed with my laptop nestled in my lap. I've been staring at Blake's friend request on Cyberjournal on and off for the greater part of the day. I've been trying to make sense of it. She specifically said she did not want to be friends online. Is she trying to confuse me? *Ugh. This woman.* Should I accept it and then message her and ask her why? Or maybe she'll call me back and when she does, I can just ask her about it then? This way I can be respectful in making sure that she's certain she wants to be Cyberjournal friends. I nod, agreeing with my decision as my gaze falls back on her profile picture. *She is one good looking specimen.* I shake my head at the fact that I just referred to her as a specimen. I study the tiny photo. It's not a selfie; it's a candid shot.

She's standing in front of her car, dangling the keys from her right hand, smiling what I can only assume is her real smile given the sparkle in her brown eyes. I enlarge the photo to better make out her figure and after I check her out for a few seconds, I look at her eyes and her smile again. I suddenly realize that I'm smiling. *No! Stop staring. Don't be that creeper.*

I click on a new tab and open a different webpage. I decide to catch up on world news. As I re-read the first sentence of the article in front of me for the fourth time, my phone buzzes breaking my almost concentration. I miss a breath. *Why?* I glance down at my cell to see who's calling. It's Blake. Without warning, my palms become moist. And once again, I'm confused. *Chill. It's just Blake.* After the third ring, I answer the call. "Hello?" I say using a very controlled tone.

"Hayden?"

A dopey grin takes my mouth hostage when she says my name and the moment I realize what's happening, I cringe. "Blake. Hi."

"Hey. I got your message."

"Right. Yes. Thanks for calling me back." Mindlessly, I switch my laptop's screen back over to Blake's profile picture so that I can see her while I listen to her.

"You're welcome. What's up?" Blake asks.

"Not much. What's up with you? How was work?"

Blake snorts on the other line. "Like you care."

"I do," I say a little too emphatically.

"It was busy. And how was your day, Hayden?"

"That's fine. Be sarcastic. I can take it," I say. "My day was alright." I think back to my conversation with Ava this morning and my heartsickness returns. "That's actually not true. It wasn't exactly the best day ever."

"Yeah. You mentioned something in your message about wanting to talk. Is that what you wanted to talk about? Your bad day?"

I sigh. "It's not that it was a bad day. It was…I'm sorting through some feelings."

There's a pause on Blake's end. I hear her swallow. "Ahh. Feelings. My favorite thing to talk about." Her voice is thick with insincerity, but it's not malicious. "What have you got? Hit me."

I'm trying to get a read on her tone. I think she's uncomfortable so I check in. "Are you uncomfortable?" I ask.

"Pfft. Me? I've got a bottle of wine in my hands, woman. I'm a lot of things right now but uncomfortable isn't one of them. I assure you. Now speak your piece or I'm going to hang up."

"Okay. Okay. It's about Ava."

I hear Blake take a long sip of her wine. "That's your best friend, right?" Blake asks.

"Correct."

"And your roomie?"

"Uh. Yeah. That too," I say.

"The one you want but can't have?"

"Yes," I say through gritted teeth. "That would be her."

"Mhmm. Okay. What's going on?"

"Remember when you accused me of being in love with her?" I ask quietly.

Blake chuckles. "It wasn't really an accusation, but go on."

I clear my throat. "So you were right. I am. I'm in love with her."

"Yeah. I know," Blake says. "Is that what you had to tell me?"

"No. There's more."

"I'm listening."

"So she's never really had much luck dating," I begin to explain. "And I thought it would be a good idea to encourage her to sign up for one of the online dating sites you swear by and—"

"Whoa!" Blake interjects. "No. Why would you do that? Why would you tell the person you're in love with to start dating?"

"Because she's not *just* the person I'm in love with. She's my best friend and so I have to be selfless and do what a good best friend would do, which is help her out."

"Right. Okay."

"Anyways," I continue. "There we are, filling out her profile and she starts telling me that she thinks she's into women."

The smallest gasp comes out of Blake. "What?"

"I know, right? Like she isn't sure how she identifies but she's pretty confident that she's not straight."

"Wow."

"My thoughts exactly."

"Then did you tell her how you really feel about her?" Blake inquires.

"No, but that's what I want to talk to you about."

The line becomes eerily silent for a long moment.

"Why me?" Blake finally asks.

"Because I can't talk to Ava since it's *about* her and you and I...we're like friends. Aren't we?"

"Dude, we just met."

"I know you're still 'feeling me out' or whatever before officially classifying us as legit friends, but, Blake, I could really use a friend right now. I know we just met but...I don't have anyone else," I practically plead.

Then I listen to the deafening sound of silence.

Chapter Thirteen

Blake

I turn Hayden's last words over in my head several times and swallow much more than a sip of wine. For some unexplained reason, I feel a feeling at the base of my stomach that resembles jealousy, but that's not possible because if I were jealous then that would mean...*No. It's not jealousy.* I make the decision to handle this situation in a way that will allow me to prove to myself that I am positively not jealous. I'll be Hayden's friend and treat her the same as I treat all of my friends...well, okay, fine. My one other friend. I inhale loud enough to let Hayden know I'm somewhat annoyed, but I'm careful not to sound too annoyed because there's no reason to be extremely annoyed unless I...and I don't.

I don't. "Okay," I say. "I'm all ears."

"Thank you," Hayden breathes into the phone.

"Yeah. Yeah. You're welcome. Now what's the problem?"

"In your opinion as a lesbian and objective bystander, do you think I should tell Ava how I feel about her?" Hayden asks.

"It depends."

"On what?"

"When Ava confided in you about her sexuality crisis, did she give you any impression that she has feelings for you that extend beyond friendship? Think. Did she say anything ambiguous? Did her body language change? Did she drop any hints?"

"Um. No."

"You're sure?" I ask.

I can practically hear Hayden frown before she says,

"Yes. I'm sure."

"Then no. I wouldn't tell her how you feel."

"Why? You said yourself that it would be painful for me to keep my feelings to myself so why don't you think I should tell her?"

"Because if she doesn't like you the way you like her and you tell her that you have feelings for her then that could freak her out. She might wonder why her *lesbian* best friend suddenly has a thing for her right after she's admitted that she's maybe not straight. It could make the dynamic between you two totally awkward...or worse than that, you could lose her as a friend," I explain. "And I'm thinking that situation would be even more painful for you. Besides, you said you were used to keeping your feelings for her to yourself."

"That was before she was questioning her sexuality. What if I tell her and she reciprocates?"

I wrinkle my brow. "Excuse me?"

"What if she does have feelings for me and she's just waiting for me to make the first move?"

Stranger things have happened. "I guess that's a possibility, but do you want to take that kind of risk? Because realistically, regardless of how she feels, once you put yourself out there, things will never be the same between you two. Your truth is always going to be there somewhere in the background and that shit's hard to ignore."

"That is risky."

I nod. "That's my point."

"Have you ever taken a risk...for love?"

I flinch and then all of my muscles tense. "This isn't about me."

"Blake, c'mon. We're friends."

"Barely."

"Still counts. Why won't you tell me?" Hayden asks.

"You're so fucking meddlesome."

"I prefer the term 'investigative'."

I roll my eyes. "Fine. Yes. I've taken a risk and it sucked. Happy?"

"Are you referring to the person who hurt you?"

"Enough with the questions, okay?" I hear the edge in my own voice.

"Okay. I'm sorry."

I sigh. "Look, you want us to be friends so I'm telling you what I would tell a friend, which is to avoid any and all potential suffering. But it's your life. If you want to take a chance, go for it. I can't stop you."

"I understand. Do you think I have a shot though?"

"I think that if Ava had romantic feelings for you then she would've figured that out by now. You guys have been in each other's lives an awfully long time. Long enough for her to know if she sees you as more than a friend. You get what I'm saying?"

Hayden's quiet for a moment. *Was I too honest? Did I upset her?*

"I do," Hayden says. "I get what you're saying."

"Hey, I could be wrong." *But I don't think that I'm wrong at all.*

Hayden takes a deep breath. "It's almost hurts worse not being able to be with her knowing she's interested in women now...and that I'm not one of those women."

I press my lips together in a thin line. *Poor girl.* I shut my eyes and shake my head. *No! Don't be sympathetic. Don't get invested. Do NOT care.* I drink more wine and quickly remind myself that Hayden and I are supposedly friends and that it's normal for friends to care about one another. Surely, I can care without getting invested. Or is caring, by default, indicative of being invested? *Ah hell.*

"Yeah. That blows," I say. "But maybe this new turn of events will help you to get over her."

"Sometimes I feel like I'm never going to get over her. I've been...under her for so many years."

"Give it time. These things take time." I stare into my empty glass. "I'm sorry that you're hurting though."

"Thanks. I appreciate that."

"Sure."

"Hey, Blake?"

I mentally prepare myself for another one of Hayden's personal questions. "What?"

"You make a good friend."

I don't mean to smile but I do. *Ugh.* "Well, duh. I'm amazing."

"That much, I've already established," Hayden says in a humorless tone.

Huh. She thinks I'm amazing. I nod to myself. *So she thinks of me then.* My heart flutters. *What the...why? No. Nooo.* I instantly press my hand to my chest in a panic as if doing so will erase the feeling I just experienced. It doesn't. That's not good. I wince at the realization that I might be in trouble. *Fuck my life.*

"You okay over there?" Hayden asks, temporarily pulling me away from my private crisis.

I clear my throat. "Yeah. I was just about to tell you not to get used to my amazingness. It was only passing through."

Hayden lets out a small laugh. "I beg to differ, but anyways, thank you. For listening and stuff."

"You're welcome."

"Also, I uh...I got your friend request on Cyberjournal but I haven't accepted it yet because it confused me and I wanted to ask you about it first."

My insides shudder. "Ask me about what?"

"About why you sent me a friend request," Hayden says. "You were pretty insistent that we *not* be Cyberjournal

84

friends and the next thing I know, I'm getting a friend request from you. It didn't make any sense. I wasn't sure if it was meant to be a prank or…?"

"No! No. It wasn't a prank." *It was completely accidental though.*

"Oh." Hayden breathes in through her nose. "So you just changed your mind?"

"Yup. That's it. I changed my mind." *That's absolutely not it.*

"I don't believe you."

"I don't care," I shoot back.

Hayden sniggers. "You're a difficult woman."

"You keep saying that."

"Because I mean it."

I shrug with my mouth. "Lucky for you that you're not my type then."

"Right." Hayden exhales. "Well do you want me to accept your friend request or not?"

Of course I want you to accept it! Accident or not, if you reject me, my pride will suffer. "Do as you please," I say impassively.

"Alright then that's what I'll do."

"Good."

"Fine."

"Fine," I repeat.

"Hey, Blake…there's one more thing."

Lord almighty. "And what might that be?"

"I wanted to ask you if…um…well, we had briefly discussed hanging out again so I thought I would ask you if that's something you wanted to do…like soon-ish?"

I smile at the way Hayden fumbled with her words. "I have to check my schedule." This is a total lie. I know my schedule.

"Yeah. For sure. Check your schedule and let me

know."

"I will."

"Cool," Hayden says. "So, enjoy the rest of your evening."

"You too."

"Thanks again."

I chuckle. "You don't have to keep thanking me, Hayden."

"Okay, but...okay. Good night then. Sweet dreams."

My breath momentarily gets trapped in my lungs. No one has ever told me to have sweet dreams. The fact that Hayden's gesture caused me to have an emotional reaction deeply disturbs me.

"Yeah. Okay. Bye," I blurt and hang up the phone.

Smooth, Blake. Real smooth. I cringe and run my fingers through my hair. *Fuuuck! I am in so much trouble.*

Chapter Fourteen

Hayden

I'm staring at the decades-old digital clock that sits atop my desk at Rose Family Auto, where I've worked as an administrative assistant for the past three years. I watch the numbers on the clock change as it hits noon. It's now officially been over fourteen hours since I accepted Blake's friend request on Cyberjournal and I've yet to hear from her in any way. No online messages, no texts, and no calls. I know this because Mr. Rose, the owner of this auto repair shop, is very lenient. I am allowed to check my cell phone whenever I want throughout my shift so long as my work gets done. With that liberty, I've been checking my phone incessantly. I don't even know why I'm being such a fanatic about this, but I am. I've only ever been fanatical about one other woman in my life, and that's Ava. But Ava's different because I have feelings for her, and with Blake, it's just that I...*It's just that I what?*

My phone vibrates against the wooden surface of my desk and I try to forget the question that's suddenly taking up way too much space in my mind. I glance down at my cell's screen. There's a text from Ava.

Hey lady, I wanted to let you know per your request this morning that my meeting with the principal and the students...AND their parents went well. He's going to review the presentation I put together. Fingers crossed! How are you?

I smile. I knew Ava would kick ass in that meeting. I pick up my phone and reply promptly.

Yay! That's awesome! I'm sure he'll be impressed and give you the green light. But I'll cross my fingers anyway. I'm alright.

Seconds after I send my message, Ava writes back.

Guess what? Some woman emailed me on Scrolling Singles! She likes my profile. She seems cool and she's totally pretty. I haven't written back yet though. I'm nervous. Advice? I feel nauseated. I shut my eyes tight for a moment and then read Ava's text again. My stomach twists even more. I know it was my idea to have her sign up for online dating but I'm second guessing my choices...and my ability to endure the outcome. I shake my head and respond.

Wow. That's exciting! Don't be nervous. Just be yourself and let it happen.

After a few seconds, Ava's reply arrives.

Okay. I'll write her back, but I can't not be nervous. Thanks for coaching me through this. You're the bestest best friend! My lunch break is over now so I gotta go. I'll keep you posted. See you at home later.

I place my phone back on the desk and cradle my head in my hands. I breathe deeply as I wait for the nausea to pass. Once it does, I nod to myself. Monday can fuck me. I'm going to Luscious tonight and if I can help it, I won't be leaving there alone.

At 4:55 that evening, I start counting down the minutes until five o' clock, when Rose Family Auto closes. Awhile back, I lost track of how many times I've checked my phone throughout the day to see if Blake reached out to me at all. She hasn't, but that doesn't stop me from checking again. Still nothing. I sigh heavily, grab my cell phone and begin composing a text message to her, but before I finish the first sentence, I delete it. I don't want to look too eager. I can be patient. *Right?*

Unexpectedly, the door behind my desk that leads out into the garage swings open and Mr. Rose steps inside the office.

"Heya, Kiddo." He smiles at me.

I swivel in my chair to face my boss. "Hey."

"It's quitting time. You got big plans for tonight?" Mr. Rose asks.

"Not really." I get out of my seat, slip my military green utility jacket on, and pluck my messenger bag from the floor beneath my desk. I sling my bag over my shoulder and turn to Mr. Rose again. "Do you?"

My boss chuckles. "Oh. I don't think I've had big plans since the seventies, but the wife made brownies and I can't ask for much more."

Awe. Well isn't that sweet. "Must be some brownies." I step out from behind my desk.

"They're the bees knees. I'll steal one for you if I can."

I laugh a little. "Thanks," I say and head for the exit.

"Hayden?"

I look over my shoulder at Mr. Rose. "Yeah?"

"Be good."

I manage to forge a smile. "Always."

"Rough day?" The familiar voice from behind the bar asks.

I glare at Connor. "Please don't hassle me. I'm not in the mood."

Connor holds up his hands as if surrendering. "I'm not hassling."

I squint at him and change the subject. "It's Monday. I thought you only worked here on the weekends."

Connor shrugs and places a napkin in front of me. "That's usually how it goes but someone called out sick and I was asked to come in. I could use the extra cash so here I am," he says with a smirk. "Vodka tonic?"

"Yes. Please."

I watch him make my drink and when he sets it down on a napkin, I can't help myself and I begin to word vomit.

"Did you know we have a mutual Cyberjournal friend now?" I ask.

Connor's brow wrinkles in confusion. "Oh yeah?

89

Who?"

"Blake Caruso."

He clears his throat. "Huh."

I scoff at his reaction. "You neglected to tell me that you knew Blake the other night when I had you send a drink over to her." I raise an eyebrow at him and take a sip of my drink. It burns.

"I didn't want to interfere."

"Oh." I purse my lips and nod. "Is that why?"

"Where are you going with this, Hayden?"

I shift my weight in my stool and lean forward a bit. "Tell me the real reason why you didn't say anything to me about knowing her."

Connor rolls his eyes. "Blake and I have a history. I was being protective."

I gasp. "Why? Did you think I was going to hurt her?"

"No. That's not it," Connor says. "Look, it's complicated so leave it alone, alright?" His cheeks suddenly rouge. Why is he embarrassed? It only takes me a second and then I understand. It's actually not complicated at all.

I tilt my head to the side thoughtfully. "You have a thing for her, don't you?"

Connor gives me a sad, tight-lipped smile. "I do. Don't you?"

My mouth drops open. *What? Why would he ask me that?* I find my voice as fast as I can. "What? No. I mean, as a friend, sure but that's it. Nothing more. Besides, I'm not even her type."

Connor chuckles. "Neither am I."

I frown empathetically. "Dude, that sucks. I'm sorry." I think of Ava. "I feel your pain."

"I know you do. And you can screw around with as many women as you'd like to dull that pain and I'll give you my blessing, but I couldn't help you out when it came to

Blake. I just didn't have it in me."

I get where he's coming from. However, because I just encouraged Ava to join a dating site, I feel defensive. "But you can't keep her from people. Don't you want her to be happy...even if it's not with you?"

"Absolutely I want her to be happy," Connor says. "And even though I didn't provide you with any ammo I have from knowing her that might've given you the upper hand, I also didn't keep you from her." He pointed to my vodka tonic. "Drink your drink, Hayden." He turned and began to walk away but I couldn't let him.

"Connor!" I called out.

He groans and heads back towards me. "What? Come on, man. I got work to do."

"What made you think I have a thing for her?"

"Because I watched you with her. You have some tells. You're an easy read, Walcott." Connor laughs to himself as he disappears to the other side of the bar. I give him the finger even though I know he can't see it. *Puh-leez. I do not have a thing for Blake. As if. Connor doesn't know jack shit.*

I swallow more of my vodka tonic and turn to the left to search the perimeter of the club. I spot a young-ish looking redhead seated alone at one of the high-top tables. Her fingers move nimbly over the keypad of her phone before she puts it down and tosses back a shot of something clear. She slides the glass to the edge of the table as if she's going to ask for a refill. I finish my own drink and rest the empty glass along with a ten-dollar bill on the bar. I eye the redhead again. She's still alone. I take a breath and ease myself off the stool. *Let's do this.*

Chapter Fifteen

Blake

"Thanks for meeting me on your lunch break," I say to Grace before I take a bite of my blueberry muffin and wash it down with a sip of my iced quad espresso.

Grace blows on her steaming hot latte. "Sure. What's going on?"

I pick off another piece of muffin and pop it into my mouth. I chew as slowly as I can to buy myself some time. *I don't really know what's going on. That's my problem.*

"Well..." I begin but stop there. I move the straw in my cup around and casually scope out the area. I focus on the painting of the Boston Commons that hangs in the hallway leading to the restrooms, which I have no need to study because I've seen it about a thousand times already.

We are sitting at a small table for two in the back of The Bean, where the town's strongest caffeinated beverages can be found. Grace and I long ago determined that there are three kinds of people in this world: non-coffee drinkers, whom we don't understand, coffee drinkers who settle for the mediocre coffee that's served at Dippin' Dough, whom we don't judge since it's the largest coffee chain in the state, and coffee drinkers who appreciate a solid, strong cup of coffee like the coffee at The Bean. We fall into the latter category, but once in a while for convenience purposes only, we've both strayed and found ourselves with a Dippin' Dough cup in hand.

It's Tuesday afternoon so the place is somewhat busy with people who've come for a mid-day pick-me-up, but most of them get their orders to go. They apparently have places to be: jobs, appointments, classes, play dates. But not me. Today is one of my days off. I definitely should get some laundry done and visit the grocery store, but I'll deal with those things later. Right now, I have something way more important to take care of. I have to say what I've been thinking or it will consume me.

From the corner of my eye, I can see Grace staring at me expectantly.

"Well what?" Grace inquires. "I have to be back at the office sometime this decade."

I pout at Grace but I also realize that I can't procrastinate any longer. I open my mouth to speak but Grace beats me to it.

"Is this about why all my calls from last night went straight to voicemail?" My best friend raises her eyebrow suspiciously. "Were you banging that chick you've been messaging with on Tap That?"

"No. That's not why I asked you here. Not exactly."

Grace smirks. "So you *were* banging that chick last night?"

I sigh. "Yes. I was. Okay? But listen, something...unexpected happened when I was...with her."

Grace's eyes widen. "Something kinky?"

I shoot Grace my notorious death glare. "No."

"Then what? Out with it."

I avert my gaze, bite my bottom lip and shake my head a little. *Maybe once I say it out loud, I'll feel better. Here goes.* "When we were...you know...I thought of someone else." I point to Grace sternly. "NOT intentionally."

Grace shrugs. "And this is problematic why?"

I groan. "Because the whole point of me fucking someone last night was so that I wouldn't think about...this certain individual but then I thought about her anyways. At the worst possible time ever." I clench the napkin in my hand. "Not to mention, that never happens to me. When I'm with someone, I'm there. I'm present. My head is in the game...NOT on another person."

Grace squints and examines my expression. "Who is this 'certain individual'? And I'm only asking because you're freaking out and you don't freak out. That's my job in this friendship," she says. "So I'm gonna guess that because of this...episode that you're having, 'this certain individual' is either someone you really like or someone you loathe, and I can't be of any assistance unless I have more information to go on."

I blink deliberately. "I can't even believe I'm going to say this out loud." I take a breath.

"It's the woman from the bar, isn't it? The one you claimed wasn't your type?"

I gape. "How did you..."

Grace taps the side of her head and says in her best Boston accent, "I'm smaht." She grins. "And you're my best friend, dummy. I know you."

"I can't be thinking about her like that."

Grace swallows a sip of her latte. "Why not?"

"Uh. Gee. There are about a million reasons why."

"Such as?"

I hold up a finger and begin counting. "One, it's not fair to the person I'm actually having sex with." I hold up another finger. "Two, she's my friend. JUST my friend." I raise another finger. "Three, she reminds me of Sarah." I stick my pinky in the air. "And lastly, she's in love with her best friend."

Grace winces. "Ooo. Yikes."

"You're telling me."

"Alright, but see it this way. First, the people you have sex with aren't people you genuinely give a shit about so no worries there. Second, friends become lovers all the time. Where do you think the plots for romcoms come from? Third, Sarah can blow herself. Seriously. She doesn't deserve the power to influence who you can and cannot be interested in."

Grace clears her throat. "As far as this woman being in love with her best friend...I don't know what to say. Is her best friend gay?"

"No but she's not straight either."

Grace nods. "Are the romantic feelings one-sided or mutual?"

"I think they're one-sided but that's just a guess based on what I've been told."

"Blake...are you thinking about...fuck, can you please tell me this person's name?"

I swipe my hand over my mouth. "Hayden."

"Hayden. Alright. So are you just thinking about Hayden in sexy ways or do you have a crush on her?"

I flinch. "Psht. Does thinking about someone even qualify as having a crush on them?"

Grace chuckles. "If you're thinking about them a lot then yeah...it does. Usually."

"I don't crush on people."

"It's okay to have crushes."

I roll my eyes. "I know that but *I* don't have crushes." I am completely not confident about that.

"Mhmm. Well, I think you have a crush and I think you know you have a crush and that's why we're here and why you're freaking out."

I frown. "Grace, I don't like this. I don't want to have a crush on anyone...especially Hayden."

Grace reaches across the table and places her hand over mine. "I know, sweetie. It's new and uncomfortable, but it's a testament to the fact that you belong to the human race, where the majority of us have, have had, or will have a crush at some point in their lifetime. Your time is now."

"How do I get rid of it?"

A quick burst of laughter escapes Grace and she quickly coughs to try to mask it. "Sorry. I didn't mean to laugh." She squeezes my hand. "You can't get rid of it. You just let it be and oftentimes, it fades on its own."

"Great," I mutter.

Grace pulls her hand back. "You could tell her how you feel."

"Nope." I drum my fingers against the table. "I'm going to get her out of my head. I don't care how many women I have to sleep with. I am not doing this crush thing. No way."

"Babe, it doesn't work that way."

"Then I'll make it work that way."

Grace shakes her head solemnly. "Okay." She glances down at her wristwatch. "I have to go back to work."

"Alright. Thanks for listening."

"Of course." Grace gets out of her seat. "After work tonight, I have to respond to an email I got from this girl I met online." She winks playfully. "So I might be a tad busy but call me if you want to talk more or whatever."

"Sure. Thanks, but I'll probably be...busy also."

"I wish you'd let your guard down," Grace says.

"And I wish you'd shut up about it."

"Prick." Grace gives me the middle finger.

I smile malevolently at my best friend and mirror her middle finger with my own. "Asshat."

Grace sniggers. "See you later, biotch." She turns and starts towards the door.

I don't want to cause a commotion so I retrieve my phone from the pocket of my jeans and text Grace.

Later, D-bag.

Then I stare at my phone and contemplate calling Hayden. I've been actively avoiding her since we spoke on Sunday. It's not that I'm trying to be cruel, but I thought that if I didn't hear from her or look at her profile online and hooked up with someone then I wouldn't think of her as much, but I was wrong. *Goddamn crush.*

Chapter Sixteen

Hayden

"Someone's been coming home late after work on the reg," Ava says to me as soon as I pass through the entrance of our apartment. She's in the kitchen moving between the cabinets and the stove. She empties a small box of rice pilaf into a pot of boiling water and gives me the side eye.

I chuckle. "I wouldn't exactly call two days 'the reg'."

Ava shrugs. "Two days in a row though. Perhaps this is going to become the new regular. How am I to know?" She stirs the rice around in the simmering water absentmindedly while she stares at me.

"Aves, it's not going to become the new regular." I take off my jacket and hang it up in its rightful spot then I step into the kitchen. "Can I help make dinner?"

Ava and I have a habit of cooking enough food to feed both ourselves and one another regardless if the other is home or not. If we both happen to be around, we usually prepare dinner together and take turns cleaning up.

"There's zucchini and a red pepper in the fridge. Get to dicing," Ava says.

"On it." I walk over to the sink and wash my hands. Then I take the vegetables out of the refrigerator. I bring them to the counter and place them on the cutting board. Ava hands me a knife and I begin my chopping project.

"Hayden, what's going on with you? You almost always come right home after work except for Fridays." Ava opens the oven door, takes a peek at the chicken that's baking inside then shuts it. She turns to me. "Maybe I'm just being paranoid but ever since I told you that I'm confused...about my sexuality...you've seemed off. Like distant or something. Are we okay, you and me?"

Tell her! "Oh. Sorry. I didn't mean to make you feel like I was giving you the shaft or anything. We're fine. I have some things I'm trying to sort out so I've been taking some time to do that after work. But yeah. We're totally fine."

Great job telling her, you idiot.

Ava arches an eyebrow at me. "Have you been sorting things out on your own...or with other women?"

I attempt a playful smirk. "What difference does it make to you?"

"Normally, I would say it doesn't make a difference, but these past two days haven't been normal. You've been acting strange. And if you *are* hooking up as a means to avoid the supposed things you have to sort out, well, that's not healthy and I'd be concerned." Ava wipes her hands on a dishcloth. "So which is it? Are you really sorting things out or are you bed hopping?"

I exhale purposefully. "Both."

Ava's forehead creases. "Come again?"

"I went out after work yesterday and today to hook up, yes. But I did it because I thought it would help me clear my head a bit."

Ava narrows her gaze at me. "Did it help?"

How do I explain this? "Um. So for me, hooking up doesn't necessarily help me figure out my feelings but it does help me forget them for a little while, which frees up some head space, which kind of rejuvenates me."

"Oh," Ava says through frown. Then she takes the tray of cut up vegetables from me, assembles them in a baking dish, and places them in the oven next to the chicken. She faces me again. "You told me once that you hooked up with women frequently because it was what you do; you didn't want to be in a relationship. You never said you did it to like escape reality."

Ugh! "Can we please talk about your day instead?

This is making me uncomfortable."

Ava gasps. "Uncomfortable? No. Since when do you have boundaries with me? We are having this conversation. You're my best friend, Hayden. I want to understand you."

"Okay. Fine. What I told you was a half-truth. I have attachment issues for sure so the idea of being in a relationship gives me the wiggins, but I'm not opposed to relationships. The main reason I chose the lifestyle that I did was to try to–as you accurately stated–escape reality."

A red shade of fury colors in Ava's cheeks. "Then you lied to me?"

I shut my eyes for a second and then meet Ava's glare. "It was more of a half-lie. I'm sorry."

"What is so terrible about your life that you have to escape it? And then lie about why you're doing what you're doing?"

Now. Tell her now. I swallow hard. "I—"

"Is this about Evie?"

Instantly, my stomach knots and my heart caves in on itself. My hands begin to tremble. We agreed not to say her name. I stare at Ava, whose complexion is pale now. She takes a step towards me.

"I'm so sorry," Ava whispers. "I shouldn't have said that." It takes me a second before I realize that Ava's arms are wrapped around me. "I'm sorry." Ava's breath tickles my ear.

I know that Ava's apology is authentic and I know that because I neglected to tell her the whole truth about myself, she had a valid reason to make the assumption she did.

"It's okay. I'm sorry I half lied to you."

Ava exhales a short, quiet laugh and loosens her grip on me. She moves back a little and our eyes meet.

"No. Don't be sorry. You're not under any obligation to share every detail of your life with me," Ava says. "I just worry about you sometimes especially after…" Her voice disappears.

"I know."

"I only worry because I love you."

Here's your chance. Tell her you're in love with her. "I love you too." *Alright. Maybe next time.*

Ava nods. "We should probably tend to the food."

"Probably. I don't think the landlord would be pleased if we burned the building down."

"True story. Though I'm thinking I might've overcooked the chicken."

I smile. Ava always overcooks the chicken. "It's all good. Not everything I eat has to be moist."

Ava gapes. "Pervert."

I grin. "Last I checked, I wasn't the only one thinking dirty thoughts about girls."

Ava grins back. "Speaking of which, I saw that you became Cyberjournal friends with Blake."

There's an unexpected flutter in my belly at the mention of Blake. *Where did that come from? Is it warm in here?* "What of it?" I ask Ava.

"You have access to all of the photos on her profile page now." Ava's eyes glint mysteriously. "Are there any good pictures of her in that sexy bra on there?"

It is definitely warm in here. "I haven't really looked at her pictures." *Lie.*

"Liarpants."

I ignore Ava's accusation and continue talking. "And I certainly don't think about Blake or her sexy bra." *Lie.* "Besides it's not even that sexy." *Lie.* Just then an image of Blake in her sexy bra flickers through my mind. *Oh my god, Hayden, have some self-control.*

Chapter Seventeen

Blake

I'm staring at the contents inside of my refrigerator, which now actually has contents to stare at so I have that going for me since I totally nailed grocery shopping a few hours ago. *What should I have for dinner?* I grab the bag of mixed greens from the produce drawer of the fridge along with the bottle of ranch dressing and use my foot to shut the refrigerator door. I put the items I'm holding on the counter and take a box of penne out of the cabinet. Boiling water is going to be the extent of my cooking tonight. Salad and pasta it is. Salad and pasta for one. Which is exactly what I want or else I'd be actively dating and dating only leads to girls breaking your heart. I'm set with that. *Thanks, Sarah.* "Bitch," I mutter as I place a pot of water on the stove and turn on the gas.

I stride over to my liquor cabinet because the six pack of porter I purchased earlier isn't as cold as I'd like it to be. *Wine or whiskey? Whiskey or wine?* The already-opened bottle of vodka catches my eye. Usually I take my vodka straight, but I could go online and Quest how to make a vodka tonic. Maybe I'll discover why it's Hayden's choice drink. Plus, this way, if she ever came over, I'd be able to make her favorite drink for her. *What?! Oh no you most certainly will not be doing that. Ever. Nope.* I shake my head and snatch the bottle of Malbec from the top shelf. Decision made.

As I start back towards the pot of boiling water, I mentally map out the rest of my night. I'm going to eat, possibly find my next potential hook-up on Tap That, and reach out to Hayden. I definitely think that the more I interact with Hayden, the easier it will be to overcome the so-called "crush" I supposedly have on her. I silently cuss out Grace and her dumb theories…even if she is maybe right. But seriously, I haven't crushed on another human since high school. And now, at twenty-nine years old, I've managed to magically develop a crush on some annoying woman I met one night at a bar? That's prosperous and it's not at all in my personality. But yet, it's happening and therefore I have to end it before it gets out of hand and Hayden becomes the only thing I think about, which I simply won't allow. Never again will one woman monopolize my head, my heart, or my body for that matter. "Nope," I quietly say as I dump half the box of pasta into the boiling water. "Never again." I nod to myself.

Nice try, Hayden. Little do you know, I have a strategy. I'm going to desensitize myself to you. "Ha!" I grin maniacally and stir the penne around. *Stupid Hayden and her stupid lip ring on her stupid full bottom lip that's utterly biteable.* I shut my eyes tightly and groan. "Lord, help me."

It's 8:32 p.m. and I'm sitting at my dark wooden, counter-height kitchen table pushing the few remaining pieces of penne around on my plate with my fork. My salad bowl is empty save for a single leaf of lettuce that's glued to the bottom by ranch dressing. My wine glass is full but that's only because I just poured myself a refill. My phone is on the table to the right of my plate. Several of my apps are open but I'm currently scrolling through the new member profiles on Tap That with my free hand. I swipe over woman after woman. *Nope. Bad fake tan. Nope. Not interested in a threesome. Nope. Those fingernails could give a lady a freaking hysterectomy. Nope. I don't want your husband to watch.* I sigh and put my fork down.

I click on the messages that have been sent to me. There are six. At random, I pick one to read. It's succinct but polite. I skim her bio. She's attractive and I approve of her taste in music. *She could work.* I reply to her message and close out the app.

Then I log into my Cyberjournal account. I disregard the number of notifications I have and go straight to Hayden's profile page. I browse her online photo album...again. *How does she have such a perfect smile?* My brow wrinkles as I continue looking. She doesn't have that many pictures. There are a couple of selfies, several photos of her and Ava at different locations around town, a photograph of the ocean, and one of her car. The picture of her car never fails to make me chuckle given the fact that her car is a jalopy. It's hard not to notice the lack of family photos. Even *I've* posted family photos.

My eyes return to the most recently posted picture of Hayden and Ava. I study Ava. She's undeniably pretty, but it's a mainstream kind of pretty: long, straight, champagne blonde hair, regular ole' blue eyes, and an oblong face. Nothing remarkable...at least not in my opinion.

I shift my gaze to Hayden, who has a very unconventional appeal to her. Unlike the color of Ava's hair, Hayden's carefully-styled bob is comprised of various shades of blonde. And differing from Ava's eyes, Hayden's blue eyes are extremely pale. The many white rays in Hayden's irises make her eyes appear almost clear. I'd be lying if I said they weren't entrancing, but I've done really well at avoiding any lengthy eye contact with her solely for that reason. Even though Hayden's smiling in the photo, her narrow chin and prominent cheekbones are easily discernible. Her facial structure is more like a diamond. Then there's that bottom lip. *Have mercy.* Hayden is anything but unremarkable.

"Aargh!" I rest my forehead on the table and rock it from side to side. *Fucking Hayden. This ends now.*

I take a deep breath, lift my head from the table and pick up my phone. I thumb through my contacts and tap on

Hayden's name as soon as it appears so as to be sure that I execute my plan without second-guessing myself. "You got this, Blake," I whisper as the phone rings in my ear.

"Well, hello," Hayden says after the fourth ring. *Goddamned butterflies.* "Hey. How are you?"

"I'm alright. I've been kind of busy these last couple of days."

Whenever I've neglected to pick up the phone when Grace calls or texts me, it's usually because I'm hooking up with someone. In the aftermath of such one-night stands, when Grace asks me why I 'ignored' her I tell her it's because I was 'busy.' I wonder if Hayden's definition of 'busy' is the same as mine in this particular instance. Something tells me it is. My stomach clenches.

I think back to the woman I spent Monday night with. "Yeah. I've been sorta tied up myself, but I had a few minutes to spare so I thought I'd give you a call."

"Awe. How generous of you," Hayden says through a chuckle.

"It comes with the territory of being amazing," I retort reflecting on her compliment from the other day.

"Ahh. I see. That makes total sense."

Something's wrong. I hear it in her voice. "Are you okay?" I ask Hayden. "You're being really quiet...you know, for...well, for you."

Hayden exhales exasperatedly. "Why are you asking? I know you don't care."

I gape. "What?! How do you know that?"

"Um. Because you're forever telling me that you don't care."

Oh. Right. "Okay. This is true, but I'm asking because I..." I close my eyes. *Because I care.* "Because I'm an inquisitive creature." I directly quote Hayden from the night we met.

Hayden laughs on the other end of the line. I smile to myself. "You're fresh," Hayden accuses.

"Sometimes, yes." Whoa. My tone was way more flirtatious than I intended.

Hayden clears her throat. *Did I make her ears blush?* After a long pause, Hayden speaks. "If you must know, it's about Ava."

Great. "Do you want to talk about it?"

"Not really. Not now at least."

"Suit yourself." I stare at my ceiling for a few seconds. *Ask her!* "Perhaps you'd want to talk about it later in the week? Like we could hang out or something?"

Hayden gasps. *"You're* inviting *me* out?"

This fucking woman. Why does she have to be so irritating? "Don't be snarky. You either want to hang out with me or you don't. It's not rocket science."

"Alright. Calm down. I was only joking."

"Please. I'm completely calm." I'm not calm at all. "I'm like fucking Buddha."

That gets another laugh out of Hayden, which evokes another smile from me. "When and where?" Hayden asks.

I already have an answer prepared. "This Friday. Eight o' clock. Meet me at Luscious."

"Um. Why Luscious?"

"Why not Luscious?"

Hayden takes a breath. "It's kind of my...um..."

"Your hunting grounds," I supply.

"Well I wouldn't quite phrase it in such animalistic terms, but..."

"Hayden?"

"Yeah?"

"Just call it what it is."

"Ugh. Fine. Yes. Luscious is where I pick up women. If I go with you then..."

I smile. "I'll cramp your style?"

"Why do you keep finishing my sentences?"

"Someone has to."

Hayden makes a noise that's part groan, part chuckle.

"Yes. Without question, you would cramp my style."

"But we'll just be two gay ladies at a lesbian bar. Lesbian friends do this sort of thing all the time. It's practically a ritual."

Hayden laughs. "I don't think it's a ritual."

I sigh. "Listen, if you want to hit on someone or someone hits on you, I won't get in the way." *Because why would that bother me? It could maybe even help expedite the demise of this idiotic crush. Right?* I chew on my lower lip. Or it could make me jealous and fuel the crush. *Shit.*

"You won't?" Hayden's question comes out sounding as unsure as I feel.

"Nope." I dramatically suck in a breath. "However, it would be terribly rude of you to dip on a friend for a stranger especially since we're not going as each other's wing women. We're going as friends." I give Hayden less than a full minute to process what I said before I continue. "I mean, frankly, and not to be cocky, I'll most likely get hit on while we're there and should that happen, I'll politely dismiss any passes made at me."

Hayden snorts. "Oh. Like how you did when I made a pass at you?"

"Exactly."

"Just so we're clear, you *are* being cocky and to say that you dismissed me politely couldn't be further from the truth."

I smirk. "Perhaps not at first but eventually I let you sit next to me and I conversed with you. That's polite."

I can almost hear Hayden roll her eyes and I ward off a laugh because we both know I'm totally messing with her.

"Why must you be so difficult?" Hayden inquires.

"Pshaw. I do believe you're being the difficult one here. I'm just being a smartass."

"I'm not being difficult."

"Prove it then. Get over yourself and meet me at Luscious on Friday," I say sternly. "This offer to hang out expires in precisely five, four, three—"

"Alright! Okay." Hayden exhales. "I'll be there."

I grin. "Cool."

"In fact not only will I be there, I won't hit on anyone while I'm there with you and when I'm hit on, I also will politely dismiss it."

I press my lips together to stifle another laugh. "You mean *if* you get hit on. Not when."

"On the contrary. I said exactly what I meant."

I'm about to make a witty remark, but I stop myself. *Stay in control of the conversation.* "Mhmm. Well, I have an early start tomorrow and a few things to take care of before I hit the sack so I'm gonna go do those things." I instantly grimace. *The sack? Really? That's the best you could do?*

"Right and I definitely don't want to stand between you and your sack." Hayden erupts in laughter.

I frown. "I'm hanging up. Goodbye."

As I move the phone away from my ear, I can faintly hear Hayden's voice.

"Goodnight, Blake," she says.

I stare at my phone, Hayden's voice echoing through my mind. Then everything is suddenly very still. Very silent. I don't want to break the silence so I just think it. *Sweet dreams, Hayden.*

Chapter Eighteen

Hayden

It's Wednesday night and I've opted not to go to Luscious after work. Instead I'm holed up in my bedroom with my laptop, typing in a question and searching for an answer that I'm not sure exists. *Can you make yourself fall out of love?* All the results that turn up are dead ends. Evidently, there are no definitive answers to the question I'm asking. I've refined my search at least a dozen times but to no avail. There are blog posts, magazine articles, and saved conversations from chat forums, but everything I come across is an opinion. And each opinion conflicts with the other. My eyes are tired from reading. I need a break. I lift my hand from the mousepad, reach for my glass of scotch and slouch back in my seat.

I take a sip of my drink while glancing over the long list of hyperlinks on my computer screen, but even from a distance, I can tell that none of them will be of any use to me. I bang my head lightly against the back of my chair. "Why is there no answer?" I raise my glass to my lips again, but the knock on my door prevents me from taking a drink.

"Entrance requested?" Ava asks from the other side of the door.

"Entrance permitted," I call back.

The door to my bedroom swings open and Ava struts through the entryway and over to where I'm sitting at my desk. I shift in my chair so that I can see her. She stops a few feet away from me. Her eyes dart from me to my drink to my computer screen. *My Quest search. Shit!* My ears begin to burn. I sit up hurriedly and snap my laptop shut. I clear my throat and casually turn back to face Ava.

"So what's up?" I ask.

Ava quirks an eyebrow at me. "Hiding something?"

I motion behind me with my thumb to my laptop.

"Pssht. No. That's just…I was uh…it was nothing."

A deep crease develops on her forehead. "You're sure it was nothing?"

"Positive."

Ava eyeballs me suspiciously "Alright." She plops down on the edge of my bed. "Can I ask you something?"

"Of course."

Ava sighs. "Okay. So I've been emailing with this woman from Scrolling Singles and it's been going well. We have a lot in common and she's cool beans. But I think she's going to ask me if I want to meet her in person soon." Ava folds her hands together. "What do I do?"

I feel like throwing up. *She's not into you, Hayden. Accept it. Be her friend like nothing's changed. You can do this.* In one gulp, I swallow back what's left of my scotch. I put the empty glass on my desk, rise up from my chair and step towards the bed. I sit next to Ava. I rub the back of my neck and take a slow, deep breath. "What do you mean? Do you not want to meet her?" I ask.

"No. I want to meet her."

My heart feels as though it's being squeezed. "Then what's the issue?"

Ava tips her back and groans. "This is stupid, I know, but I'm scared." She looks at me. "I've never been with a woman. Not even a kiss."

I afford my friend a small smile. "It's not stupid to be scared."

Ava scoffs. "Easy for you to say. You're experienced."

"That doesn't mean I don't get scared or nervous around women I'm interested in." *Like you.*

"Like Blake?" Ava grins.

110

My belly flops. *Oh come the hell on.* "Psht. No," I say unconvincingly.

"How does it feel?"

My brow wrinkles. "How does what feel?"

"Kissing a girl."

Immediately, my palms dampen. I become exceedingly aware that there isn't much space between us. I can smell her coconut scented shampoo. Quickly, I divert my attention to the rug beneath my feet. *Don't think about kissing. Don't think about mouths. Don't think about lips.* Out of nowhere, an unsolicited image of Blake's plump, shimmering lips flashes through my head. *Not helping! What the fuck is happening to me? Okay. Focus.* I inhale and shift my gaze to meet Ava's watchful eyes. "Kissing a girl," I start as I rub my palms on the knees of my cargo pants. "It feels…awesome."

Ava frowns. "Hayden, please."

I nod. "Alright. But remember, I can only speak from *my* experience."

"I know."

I swallow. "Okay. It's soft. Women are soft. Their lips are soft. Their skin is soft. It's just an amazing feeling."

Ava's eyes are wide. She bites her bottom lip and smiles shyly. "That does sound awesome."

"It is."

Ava's smile dissolves. "And sexy."

A drop of perspiration trickles along my hairline. "Uh huh."

I stop breathing altogether when Ava places her left hand on my right cheek and inches closer. *What is she doing?* Before I can protest even half-heartedly, Ava's lips brush over mine. A chill runs across my entire body. I close my eyes and she kisses me again. Everything comes to a standstill.

111

Everything is spinning. I kiss her back.

I am not sure how long Ava and I have been kissing for when suddenly I feel the absence of her warm lips. Her hand is still on my cheek. I slowly open my eyes and Ava is staring right back at me, her expression filled with uncertainty. *Shit.*

"I...I don't...I didn't." Ava blinks deliberately and moves her hand away from my face. "I'm sorry."

No! I go to grab Ava's hand but she stands up too fast. "It's okay. You don't have to be sorry."

"I'm gonna go. I need to think." Ava shakes her head and starts to exit my room, but stops in the doorframe and glances over her shoulder at me. "I am. I'm sorry."

I open my mouth to speak but she leaves and closes the door behind her. "Aargh!" I rest my elbows on my knees and bury my face in my hands. *Is our friendship ruined now? Does she regret it? What does she need to think about it?* Then it hits me and I raise my head. My eyes fall on the framed photograph of the two of us on the day she received her Master's Degree. Ava's wearing her cap and gown, holding her diploma in one hand and the bouquet of flowers I gave her in the other hand. My arm is around her and she's leaning into me as I snap the picture. I study our smiles, our body language. I exhale. *What if she does like me? That has to be it. Why else would she kiss me?* I nearly jump to my feet, about to go to Ava to finally declare my feelings for her and hopefully ease whatever worries she might be having but once my hand is wrapped around the doorknob, I pause. I don't want to encroach on her personal space if she needs to process. I sigh and lean my back against the door. I take my phone out of my pants pocket and send Ava a text.

Aves, you don't owe me an apology. You did nothing wrong. Are we okay? I watch my phone, silently pleading for

Ava's reply. My heart skips when my phone finally buzzes in my hand with Ava's response.

We're okay. I just have a lot of feels right now. We'll talk later. Goodnight. I smile at the thought of Ava's feels being for me. *Goodnight.* I put my phone back in my pocket, walk over to my desk and open my laptop. I re-read the question I had typed in my search bar earlier: *Can you make yourself fall out of love?* Confident that the question is completely irrelevant now that everything has changed, I erase my search. I lie back on my bed, my arms behind my head and close my eyes. I play it over in my mind.

We're sitting on the edge of my bed, her hand is on my cheek and she begins to lean in. Her glossy, bee-stung lips about to graze mine, her golden brown eyes locked on mine. *Wait. What?* My eyes shoot open, my heart's pounding. Ava doesn't wear lip gloss and she doesn't have brown eyes. Blake does.I take a calming breath. Clearly, I'm exhausted and my sanity is slipping because there's no rational reason for Blake to be making an appearance in my fantasies. None. "None," I repeat aloud, desperately trying to reassure myself.

Chapter Nineteen

Blake

"Blake," Kendall whispers.

I turn to my right to look at my colleague. "What?"

"I just talked a woman into buying nine pairs of our new boxer briefs."

I smile. "Great!"

Kendall shrugs. "Thanks, but I think she wants to buy some new bras too and I'm not sure what to suggest. Her style is...um...I think she might be...you know...not completely feminine...like at all. I'm not trying to be a stereotyping bigot but I'm thinking maybe she's..." Kendall stares at me helplessly, her eyes wide and begging me to finish her sentence.

"Queer?" I offer.

Kendall lets out a relieved sigh. "Yeah." She nods. "What should I recommend?"

I tuck my lips behind my teeth to keep from laughing and clear my throat. "Not all queer women prefer the same undergarments."

"I know but..."

"Where is she?"

Kendall tips her head slightly to the left. "By the flannel bottoms. Buzz cut. Men's leather jacket. Camo-colored khakis. Work boots."

I discreetly glance over Kendall's shoulder, spot the woman she's referring to, and then turn my attention back to the perfume display I had been organizing. *Definitely a hundred-footer.* "You know the drill. Compliment what she's already chosen and then ask her what she's looking for in a bra. If she has an answer, awesome. If she doesn't know, suggest the plainest, most basic bra we have. Nothing too colorful. Nothing frilly. Okay?"

Kendall smiles. "Okay."

"Now go make that sale." Oblivious to the fact that Kendall hasn't walked away yet, I squirt the tiniest bit of Sorcery on my wrist from the test bottle.

"I thought Pixie Dust was your favorite," Kendall says. *Oh shit.* I promptly place the bottle in its rightful spot. "It is, but this one's a close second and I wanted to make sure the pump worked." *That the pump worked?! Because that's brilliant.*

Kendall squints at me. "Right."

Also, I have this mega crush on woman who wears this perfume so I'm going to be a super creep and sniff my wrist throughout the day. You know, the same way any person slowly losing a grip on reality would do.

I tilt my head in Buzz Cut's direction. "Go get it."

Kendall grins. "I will," she says and parades back towards the customer. I know she'll make the sale. Kendall and Julie are my top two saleswomen. They're both still in college, young and gullible at times, but they're fast learners and I'm hoping to help them climb the company ladder so that they stay with the store after they graduate. I'm also not naïve and I'm aware that I'm an anomaly; happy with my career in retail.

From the corner of my eye, I watch Kendall lead Buzz Cut to the cash registers, two bras in her hand. I smile to myself, lift my wrist to my nose and inhale. If I smell Hayden, it will help with the desensitization process. It's all part of the plan. "Totally," I mutter to myself as I rearrange the perfume bottles on the showcase table.

By six o' clock that Thursday evening, I'm in the office finalizing the schedule for next week. I take the final bite of my granola bar and toss the wrapper in the trash can. I triple check the schedule I've created, email a copy to headquarters and print out another copy to post by the time clock for the employees to see. Since this is technically my break, I've had my phone on my desk for the past forty minutes. Before I lock it back up and head to the sales floor again, I read through the messages I received on Tap That. Only one woman seems moderately interesting. I'm about to reply and ask her if she'd like to meet up with me later tonight, but I catch a whiff of Hayden emanating from my left wrist. My insides somersault and my fingers momentarily refuse to move. I shut my eyes and wish away the thought of Hayden. When I open my eyes, I can still visualize her in that freaking black button down shirt. In her snapback. In nothing at…*Whoa! No!* I shake my head. "Pull yourself together," I hiss. Then I log out of the app, put my phone in my locker and make my way to the bathroom to wash the perfume from my wrist.

Between covering my employees' breaks, assisting customers, sending sales reports to corporate and dealing with one mishap in the stock room, which resulted in Julie being attacked by a dozen teddies, the last four hours of my shift race by. As I'm pulling my car out of the mall parking lot, I glimpse at the clock above the radio dials. It's 11:32 p.m. I groan. I'm equal parts exhausted and tense. Sex usually relaxes me, but so far, every time I've hooked up with someone this week in an attempt to dull my thoughts of Hayden, I've only ended up thinking of her more, which stresses me out. It doesn't matter that I have no real human connection with the women I sleep with, I don't feel right having sex with someone whilst fantasizing about someone else.

I'm suddenly aware of how tightly I've been squeezing the steering wheel when a cramp surges through both of my hands. *Damnit.* I take my left hand off the wheel and give it a little shake. Just then my phone pings. I know that sound. It's a notification from Tap That. *Ignore it.* When I reach the next red light, I take my cell out of my purse and look at the notification. *Alright. Ignoring it didn't go so well.* It's a message from a woman who's nearly a decade my senior. She's good-looking with dark features and even darker eyes. More importantly, her message is concise.

Hi. I read your profile. If you're around tonight, I'm down to fuck. No strings attached.

I glance up at the light. It's still red. I chew on my bottom lip as I consider this stranger's proposition. This woman couldn't look any less like Hayden if she tried. Maybe this will be the one that frees me from the image of Hayden. It has to. Right? I type up a quick response before the light changes.

Where do you want to meet?

Chapter Twenty

Hayden

I knock on the slightly ajar bathroom door.
"Aves? Can I come in?"
Suddenly, the door is pulled open all the way. Ava waves me in, a toothbrush in her mouth. She's in skinny jeans, a stylish over-sized knit sweater and brown wedge boots. Her long, blonde hair is down save for the loose, horizontal braid that's keeping the side locks off her face. My heart collapses. She's dressed for a date.

Ava spits out a mouthful of white foam, rinses and then dabs around her lips with a towel. After she hangs the towel back on the rack, she regards me cautiously.
"Going out?" Ava asks me.

I realize my outfit is a dead giveaway: slim straight dark wash men's jeans, a fitted white button down tucked in and suspenders. It's only now that I'm beginning to second-guess my attire. I might be too overdressed for meeting up with a friend.

I motion to Ava. "I could ask you the same thing?"

Ava turns her attention to the mirror above the sink that also acts as a cabinet and attempts to tame a few stray strands of hair. Once she's satisfied with her appearance, she faces me. "I have a date...with that woman I've been messaging with."

A sharp pain rips through my chest. *Ugh.* "Oh. Wow. That's...wow."

Ava smiles shyly. "And what about you? Why are you all dolled up?"

I am not dolled up. "Psht. I'm not dolled up."

"Are too."

"Am not. It's Friday night. I'm just going to hang out with Blake."

Ava laughs. "Blake, huh?"

"Why are you laughing?"

"You really want me to believe that you and Blake are just going to 'hang out'?"

I gasp. "Yes, because that's really all we're doing." *And I'm in love with you and we kissed so...*

Ava quirks an eyebrow at me. "Mmhmm."

I take out my hair product, which is what I came in here for.

Ava inhales dramatically. "Perfume *and* hair product."

"I just want to look presentable."

"Suuuure."

I roll my eyes and Ava giggles. This is our first real interaction since our kiss. It feels normal. There doesn't seem to be any awkwardness. *This is good.*

Ava clears her throat. "I'm sorry I've been avoiding you since...since we kissed."

Aaannd it's awkward. I unintentionally stare at her lips before I meet her eyes. "It's okay. I know you needed space to process."

Ava nods and squats down in front of me. She takes my hands in hers. *Is she going to kiss me again? Please let her kiss me again.*

"You know I love you, right?" Ava says.
Nothing good ever follows those words as far as my experiences have taught me.

"Yeah. I know." I speak so softly that I can barely hear myself.

"I shouldn't have kissed you. I'm wicked sorry."

My mouth opens a little as all the air escapes my lungs. *Don't cry.* I clench my jaw to keep my expression hard.

"Why are you sorry?"

119

"Because you're my best friend, not a science experiment. I was in the moment listening to you talk about what it's like to kiss another woman and I let my curiosity get the best of me. I should've restrained myself."

No! Don't restrain yourself. "It's okay."

"It's not though. It's not okay." Ava begins to stand up but I tighten my grip on her. This is it. I'm going to tell her.

"Wait." I swallow when Ava resumes her position in front of me. My mouth is so dry.

Ava glances at our clasped hands and then looks me in the eyes. "What?"

"I...um. I liked it." *I'm going to throw up.* "I liked our kiss."

Ava gapes and her brow wrinkles. "What do you mean?"

"I've been keeping something from you since we were freshmen in college and I have to tell you now or I'm never going to tell you and if I don't tell you then I might regret it for the rest of my life, but I'm scared so just listen, okay?" I'm not sure how I said all of that in one breath, but I did.

I watch as the color drains from Ava's face. She knows what I'm about to say.

"Hayden—"

"I'm in love with you," I blurt before she can stop me. "I've been in love with you for years, but I always thought you were straight, so it was pointless to tell you how I felt but then you had this whole self-discovery thing and..."

Ava lets go of my hands and stands up. "And what?" She holds out her arms. "You'd tell me and I'd realize that all along, I've had feelings for you too? Hayden, that's not how it works."

"I understand that, but—"

Ava places her hands on either side of her head and shakes it. "No! Hayden, no. We're best friends. You're like

120

family to me. And now you're sitting here telling me that for the entire time we've known each other, you've had romantic feelings for me. Is that the only reason you stuck around in my life? Have you been waiting around this whole time secretly hoping that one day I'd want to be your girlfriend?" She pauses for a moment and then her eyes widen. "Oh my god! Have you been sleeping with all those women to make me jealous or something? Jesus, Hayden! Has our whole friendship just been one big long game to you?!" She quickly swipes away the tear that leaked from her right eye.

"Ava, no!" I jump to my feet. I reach out to latch onto her arms, but she steps back and points at me.

"Don't," Ava says.

"I love you no matter what. I've stuck around because I love you as a person, not because I'm in love with you. You *are* the only person in my life who I love. You know that. I'm sorry I kept my feelings a secret."

Ava glares at me. "Tell me truthfully, did you decide to confess your feelings for me because you thought you had a chance with me? Like my acknowledging that I'm into girls somehow automatically means that I'd be into you?"

Yes. "Not exactly. I—"

"Stop!" Ava takes another step backwards towards the bathroom door. "I don't want to hear it. I can't with you right now."

"You can't what with me right now? What does that mean? You can't be my friend? My roommate? Talk to me. Please."

"I don't know." Ava's bottom lip trembles. "I'm really sorry I kissed you...if it gave you the wrong impression, but you were never a game to me."

"You were never a game to me either. I swear!" I'm sweating now. "Just tell me we can still be friends."

121

Ava does another one of her slow head shakes. "I don't know."

"Ava."

"I'm going. I have a date that I don't want to be late for." Ava turns and walks out of the bathroom. I listen to her boots click along the floor of our apartment all the way to the front door. I hear the jingle of her keys.

"I'm sorry!" I yell as the door to our apartment slams shut. I close my fists and smash them against the bathroom wall. "Fuck!"

Chapter Twenty-One

Blake

It's 7:47p.m. when I walk through the entrance of Luscious. My heart is beating faster than I'd prefer as I scan the vicinity for Hayden. *Why must I have a crush on her? It's so annoying.* Aside from being frustrated by the case of jitters I'm experiencing—a rarity for me— I'm also unsure of my outfit. How exactly does one dress to meet up with someone who is just a friend? At first, I chose articles of clothing that I'd wear whenever I hung out with Grace, but that left me feeling underdressed because as much as I know that this is a casual get together, there is still a part of me that wants to pique Hayden's interest. After much deliberation, I settled on dark blue jeggings, my black, off-the-shoulder chiffon top with wide, billowy sleeves, a black, velvet choker to draw attention to my neckline, and my black leather buckled ankle boots. I kept my hair down. Minimal makeup per usual. However, because I accidentally slept in my contacts and nearly burned my eyes out of my head, I am forced to wear my glasses. This, I am not pleased about, but I just have to deal.

Luscious is no more busy than I'd expect for a Friday night, but it's not overly crowded either. There's a few women surrounding the pool table towards the back, a cluster of younger twenty-somethings on the dance floor, and only two of the tables are occupied. The bar itself, on the other hand, is swamped. I catch a glimpse of Connor as he reaches for a half-filled bottle of clear alcohol. In spite of myself and all my gay glory, I have to admit that he is one good-looking fella. I smile to myself and continue searching the faces of all the patrons at the bar.

When my gaze falls upon that familiar blonde head of hair, my stomach tumbles. Hayden's facing front, so she doesn't see me standing there, several feet to her right, staring at her like a dork. I steel myself and start for the bar. I push past a group of older women, who don't seem to mind judging by the way they gawk at me.

One of them is even brash enough to whistle under her breath and say, "Aren't you a fine piece of ass." I stop dead in my track. *Oh the hell you didn't*. I turn and glare at Smart-mouth McGee.

"And aren't you a disgusting piece of shit." I wink at her, pivot on my heels and continue towards the bar. In the distance, I can hear the chuckles of her friends. I smirk, satisfied with myself.

Finally, I reach the bar. There are six people and seven barstools separating me from Hayden, who still hasn't noticed my arrival. I wave down Connor, who grins as soon as he sees me. He slides a bill across the counter to a customer then comes over to me.

"Blake, hi."

"Hey. How are you?"

"Good." He inhales through his nose. "You look good." He blushes.

I smile. "So do you."

Connor's blush deepens. "Um. Thanks. Where's Grace?"

"I didn't come here with Grace. I'm meeting a friend."

Connor's brow wrinkles. "Really?"

I tilt my head in Hayden's direction. "Really."

Connor glances at Hayden then looks at me. "Ahh. See? I told you she's cool."

Yep. She's cool alright. And I have a major lesbian hard-on for her. "Yeah. Whatever," I say. "Can you do me a solid?"

"Sure. Name it."

"Would you kindly send her a vodka tonic but don't tell her it's from me." When I feel the heat creeping up my cheeks, I take my wallet out of my purse to try to hide my face. I fish for twenty-dollar bill, pull it from my wallet and hand it to Connor. "Please."

Connor snickers and pushes the money back at me. "It's on the house."

I place everything back inside my purse and offer Connor a small nod. "Thank you."

Connor smiles at me then walks off. I watch him begin to make Hayden's drink. I start stepping carefully towards Hayden. I pause by the empty barstool beside her, which I'm assuming she's saving for me. *Awe. Well that's thoughtful.* She's folding and unfolding the napkin in her hands, tuned out to her surroundings...myself included. I use this moment to take her in. She's swapped her black button down for a white short-sleeved button down. I can barely make out the ribbed tank top beneath it. I notice more black ink on her right bicep through the fabric of her shirt, but I can't tell what exactly the tattoo is of. I make a private bet with myself that it's most likely something super gay. The thought makes me smile as I keep cruising her. I stop smiling. Hayden's wearing suspenders. *My god. She's wearing suspenders.* Instantly I imagine Hayden in those slim-fitting jeans she's rocking, the tank top, those suspenders, and nothing else. My whole body warms over. *Clean thoughts. Clean thoughts.* I take a breath and swallow. Just then Connor sets the vodka tonic in front of Hayden and vanishes from sight. Hayden eyes the drink with a confused expression and that's when I make myself known.

"Aren't you gonna drink that?"

Hayden smiles before she turns to me and as soon as she does, as soon as her eyes meet mine, my heart misses a beat. *Collect yourself.*

125

Hayden blatantly eyes the length of me and whether it's a conscious act or not, she licks her lips. I smirk at her. "See something you like?"

Hayden lowers her head a bit and shakes it while chuckling softly. She looks up to face me again.

"You know I find you attractive. We met because I hit on you. Remember?"

"Oh. I just thought you hit on me because I have a vagina." I grin.

Hayden feigns surprise and drops her jaw. "You have a vagina? Well, shit."

A small laugh escapes me. "Hello, Hayden."

Hayden grins as she gets out of her seat. Now we're standing face to face and it takes every ounce of willpower within me not to grab her by her suspender straps and pull her closer.

"Blake." Hayden regards me with a nod then motions to the vacant barstool she had been sitting next to. "I saved you a seat."

"Why thank you." I can't help myself. I reach out with my left hand and pinch one of her suspender straps between my forefinger and thumb. I can feel Hayden stiffen. If I didn't know that she was in love with another woman, I'd swear she was into it. *If only.* "Suspenders, huh?" I let go of the strap.

Hayden presses her mouth into a tight smile. "Suspenders."

"How gay of you." I smile and sit on the stool that Hayden saved for me.

Hayden laughs and takes the seat beside me.

"Can I order a beer for you?" Hayden asks.

"Thanks, but I got it." I crane my neck to where Connor is and wait for him to look my way. It takes all of ten seconds. He smiles at me. I return the gesture and hold up one finger. He takes a bottle of beer from the cooler and

126

walks over to where Hayden and I are. He places the beer in front of me and pops off the top.

"Anything else?" Connor asks me.

"This will be all for now, Kind Sir."

Connor's eyes flicker between me and Hayden.

"Okay." He strolls back to the other side of the bar.

I take a sip of my beer. I can see Hayden staring at me through my peripheral vision. I can feel it. I swallow and turn to her.

"All you have to do is look at him and he knows you want a beer?" Hayden asks.

I shrug. "The boy knows me. I told you, we go back."

Hayden purses her lips. "Do you think he still has a thing for you?"

I almost spit out a mouthful of porter. "Ha! Nooo. He knows I'm a lesbian."

"So? People have things for people they can't have all the time."

I don't know if this is about Connor anymore or about Hayden's feelings for Ava. I internally frown at the sudden realization that what Hayden just verbalized could easily pertain to me as well. *Fucking crush. Go the hell away already.*

"Connor doesn't like me like that," I say.

"Okay." Hayden takes a drink of her vodka tonic the raises the glass. "Thanks for this by the way."

I lift my beer bottle and clink it against Hayden's glass. "You're welcome by the way." We both drink.

"I didn't know you wore glasses."

I curl my upper lip and stick my tongue out of the side of my mouth. "Yeah. I've been wearing glasses since I was in third grade."

Hayden nods. "Are you near-sighted or far-sighted?"

I snort. "I'm barely sighted." Hayden laughs and I smile.

"Technically, I'm near-sighted." I swivel in my stool so that I'm facing Hayden. I take off my glasses. "Like I can see you perfectly fine right now but if you were further away, you'd be fuzzy." I then put my glasses back on.

Hayden shifts in her seat, her position mirroring that of my own. Our knees are touching.

"Well, for what it's worth, they work for you," Hayden says and the tips of her ears crimson. I pretend not to notice. Instead, I arch an eyebrow.

"Oh yeah? And are they working for you?"

Hayden's ear-blush makes its way to her cheeks. She coughs. "What? No."

"Mmhmm."

Hayden rolls her eyes. "Your arrogance is really off-putting."

I stick my tongue out again but this time it's at Hayden. "*You're* really off-putting."

Hayden snickers, but then her expression turns solemn. "Can I confide in you about something? Because we're friends now and stuff."

I put my beer down, but keep my focus on Hayden. "Sure."

Hayden takes a long drink of her vodka tonic then sets the glass on the bar. She looks at me with cloudy eyes. "When you and I talked on the phone earlier this week, I was bummed out because Ava had told me that she's been messaging regularly with this one particular woman from Scrolling Singles. I was processing…you know, the idea of her dating…women." Hayden drops her gaze and fidgets with the faux leather cuff around her left wrist.

"Women who aren't you?" I contribute.

Hayden returns her eyes to my face. "Yeah."

I frown. *Okay. Be a friend.* I place my hands on her knees. *Is this too intimate for friends? Well too late now anyways.* "I'm sorry."

Hayden shakes her head. "It gets better."

I raise my eyebrows. "How do you mean?"

"A few days ago, Ava kissed me."

There's a painful twist in my gut. "Oh. Wow."

Hayden closes her eyes and pinches the bridge of her nose. "Ugh. I was such an idiot."

I don't think, I just reach up and gently ease Hayden's hand away from her face. "Look at me." Hayden's breath catches when I touch her. She shakily exhales. Then she stares at me. I can't read her expression. I immediately draw my hand back.

"I thought the kiss was real," Hayden continues. "I thought maybe she had feelings for me, but we talked about it right before I came here to meet you and she apologized for it, saying it was a mistake and then...and then like a moron, I tell her how I feel about her..."

I wince.

Hayden grits her teeth. "I fucking told her I was in love with her. You told me not to tell her and I went ahead and did it anyways and now she's pissed at me. She's questioning the validity of our entire friendship. Christ. I don't even know if she wants to be friends with me anymore. She thinks I only stayed friends with her because I wanted to get with her and that's not it." Hayden swallows back her sorrow. "That's not it. You believe me, don't you?"

I nod. *Should I hug her? This seems like a hugging moment.* I second-guess my instincts and give Hayden's right shoulder a sympathetic squeeze instead.

"Yes. I believe you," I say.

"Thank you."

If Hayden were any other woman emotionally unraveling before me, I'd find a way to comfort her in a bed somewhere, but she's not any other woman. She's my friend. Sure, she's my friend who I want to have sex with but my friend nonetheless. I remove my hand from Hayden's shoulder and reach into my purse. I pull out that twenty-dollar bill from earlier and place it on the bar beneath my empty beer bottle. I tap Hayden's leg. "Come on. Let's get out of here." *Okay so that sounded far more seductive out loud than it did in my head.* I inwardly cringe.

Hayden studies my features for a moment. I'm hot everywhere under her scorching, crystal blue stare. *Stay cool.* "Okay," Hayden says.

Alright. Awesome. She's coming with me. Now where the frig do I take her? I dismount from my stool and offer Hayden my hand. I convince myself that it only makes sense for us to hold hands so that we don't lose each other as we weave through the crowd towards the exit. Almost. I almost convince myself. *Good god, what am I doing? What if she doesn't take my hand? Then I'll really look like a cool kid. Are my palms sweating? Aargh! Fuck my life.*

Chapter Twenty-Two

Hayden

I slide my hand into Blake's. Her skin is soft. I can't tell whose palms are damp—mine or hers. Probably mine. When Blake offered me her hand, it caught me by surprise. She doesn't strike me as the hand-holding type. The gesture was sweet...and if I'm to be honest, kind of sexy. Yep. The sweaty palms are definitely mine. Blake gives me a light tug, pulling me off my stool and begins marshaling me towards the exit of Luscious. I have no idea where we're going and I couldn't care less because the second Blake held my hand, she became the only thing I could feel. I'm not allowing myself to ask myself why that is. Not now at least.

Blake leads me all the way to her car and then she lets go of my hand. She turns to me. "I understand if you want to call it a night," Blake says.

"I'm not ready to go home yet."

"Are you okay with leaving your car...with leaving Leela here?"

I smile. "Yeah. She'll be fine."

Blake points to her sedan with her thumb. "Then I suggest you get in."

"You're kinda bossy." *It's hot as fuck.*

Blake smirks. "It drives the ladies crazy."

I give her a tight-lipped smile. "Right." Then I round the car to the passenger's side. If I had stood there any longer, she would've detected my blush. Once we're both inside the vehicle, Blake starts the engine and motions to the radio.

"I'm not equipped with mixed tapes. Sorry. But there are a few CDs in the glove compartment. There's also satellite radio so the stations are limitless. Feel free to play DJ."

"Seriously?"

Blake raises an eyebrow at me. "Um. Yes. Why wouldn't I be serious?"

"Because appointing someone with the responsibility of playing DJ in a car that's not theirs is huge deal."

Blake chuckles. "I trust you." She checks the rear and side-view mirrors and then pulls out of her metered parking space and on to the road.

I rummage through Blake's disc collection, impressed by her diverse taste in music. I make my choice and slip Bass Daddy's debut rap album into the CD player. I crank the volume.

"Aw yeah!" Blake bobs her head to the beat of the drum machines backing Bass Daddy's lyrics and when the chorus starts, we both begin rapping in time to the music, smiling hard but unwilling to laugh at the risk of disrupting our flow. We kill it.

"Yasss!" I hold my fist out to Blake when the chorus is over and she bumps her fist against mine. It's only after our fist bump that we burst out laughing. Blake has the best laugh I've ever heard. No question.

Blake's waving her fork in front of my face.

"Just try it," she says.

Blake and I are sitting across from one another in booth inside of Adrianna's Pie House, a quaint diner I never even knew existed right on the outskirts of town. It's brightly lit, and on the walls next to each table hangs a framed photograph. Some of the pictures are of people, others are of animals, but most of them are scenic: a night sky, a sun rising over the ocean, a snow-drenched hiking trail, the entrance of a subway stop in downtown Boston. This place undoubtedly has a cozy vibe to it.

I stare at the small chunk of apple pie on Blake's fork.

"No thank you."

Blake's eyes widen. "Hayden, you *have* to try it. I cannot believe you've never had apple pie. It's practically a crime."

I chuckle. I'm thoroughly enjoying Blake's enthusiasm for apple pie.

"How about this," Blake says. "If you don't like it, I'll do anything you want."

Automatically, my mind undresses Blake. *Jesus.*

"You'll do anything, huh?"

"Yup."

"You have an awful lot of confidence in apple pie," I say.

"This is not just apple pie. It's *Adrianna's* apple pie and it's bomb."

I squint at the morsel of pie on Blake's fork again. Blake moves the fork closer to my mouth.

"Open up," Blake lilts.

I smile.

"You know you want a foodgasm." Blake wiggles her eyebrows suggestively.

Welp. This officially sucks harder than I thought. Not only is Blake incredibly sexy but she's also crazy cute. I roll my eyes for effect even though I'm not annoyed and open my mouth.

Blake grins. "You won't regret this life decision." She inches the fork gently into my mouth. I take the bite, chew slowly and swallow. It's probably one of the best things I've ever tasted. But I bet Blake tastes pretty fucking amazing. *Whoa! Keep your head in the game.*

Blake slowly pulls her fork away from my lips and stares at me expectantly.

"It's really good," I admit.

Blake beams. "Yeah?"

133

"Totally."

"Noice!" She nods while she takes a bite of pie herself.

"So do you eat out a lot?" *Oh god! What?* I shake my head emphatically. "No. Not what I...no." Blake's already laughing. "Here. Do you eat out here a lot?"

Blake answers through the ghost of her laugh. "I know what you meant. I wouldn't say I come here a lot per se. About once or twice a month."

"How did you find this place?" I ask.

"I'm chummy with the owner." The mere thought of Blake and Adrianna having sex makes me want to regurgitate my bite of apple.

"Chummy like how?" I try to maintain a nonchalant tone.

Blake smirks at me. "Is that jealousy I'm hearing in your voice?"

Fail. "Psht. No." *Please don't let my ears blush.*

Blake arcs an eyebrow at me, unconvinced. "If you say so."

"Have you forgotten? I'm inquisitive."

"No. I haven't forgotten." Blake puts her fork down and takes a sip of water. "We never slept together if that's really what you're asking."

I scrunch up nose. "That wasn't what I was asking."

"Mhmm." Blake points to me. "Your ears said otherwise."

Damnit.

"Anywho," Blake continues. "We used to work together. After she left to start her own business, we remained friendly."

"She worked at Undercover with you?"

"She did. She was good at it too but it's not what she wanted for her life. And now she gets to do what she loves."

134

"Good for her."

"Yeah. I'm proud of her." Blake glimpses at the half-eaten slice of blueberry pie on my plate. "How's your food?"

"Hands down the best blueberry pie I've ever had."

Blake grins. "Excellent."

I force a smile and nod.

Blake exhales. "Hayden, I brought you here because it has a more conversation-friendly environment than a club so if you want to talk about it…about Ava, I'm listening."

"I'm not sure if there's anything left to say." *Except for that I'm a big fuck up.*

"Okay. You don't have to say anything. I won't push."

Blake unexpectedly helps herself to a forkful of my pie. She smiles as she chews. "Mmm. Tasty."

I gape at her.

Blake swallows her food. "What? We're friends. Friends share…do they not?"

A genuine smile escapes me. "They do."

"Alright then. So, *friend*, is blueberry your favorite kind of pie?"

My brow creases. "I guess. Yeah." I meet Blake's eyes. "But apple is quickly climbing the ranks."

"Hell yes it is!" She holds out her closed hand and we fist bump again. I laugh.

"And would you say pie is your favorite dessert?" Blake asks.

"I would not because ice cream is my favorite dessert."

"Huh. What flavor?"

"Chocolate chip cookie dough is my go-to."

"Premium choice."

"Thank you," I say, forcing the thought of licking ice cream off of Blake's lingerie-adorned body out of my mind. "Is pie your favorite dessert?"

"No. Pussy is." Blake deadpans and I choke on my own spit. Through a fit of laughter, she asks me if I'm okay. I catch my breath and glare at her.

When Blake's laugh fades into a proud smirk, she holds up both of her hands innocently. "What?"

I give Blake a grievous side-eye. "You. You're fresh."

"So you've said and I never disagreed." Blake winks at me and when she does I feel my pulse between my legs. My cheeks burn and the tips of my ears warm over. *Fucking hell.* I wait for Blake to comment on my ear blush but she doesn't. Alternatively, she is kind enough to assume the role of oblivious on-looker.

"Okay. In all seriousness, yes. Pie is, in fact, my favorite dessert."

I nod, glance at the crumbs left on Blake's plate and then I look up at her. "Apple?"

Blake smiles. "What gave it away?"

I breathe out a short, half-hearted laugh through my nose. I begin toying with my wrist cuff.

"Something I said?" Blake inquires.

I wipe my mouth with my hand and meet Blake's eyes. "No. I um...thanks for bringing me here. It's a good distraction...not quite the distraction I'm accustomed to, but a welcome change."

"I'm glad." Blake crosses her arms and rests them on the table. "So what say you? Are you ready to go home now?"

Blech! Absolutely not. However, I don't want to burden Blake. What if she isn't even enjoying my company?

"I'll pass on going home but you can drive me back to my car. I'll just go somewhere for a bit. I don't expect you to keep me company all night. That'd be no fun for you," I say.

"I think you should let me be the one who decides what is and isn't fun for me."

I press my lips together and nod. "You're right. I apologize."

"Apology accepted." Blake grabs her purse. "C'mon. Let's go."

"Where are we going?"

"I'm going to the counter to pay the bill."

I squint at Blake. "Okay. After that, where are we going?"

Blake gives me a mischievous grin. "I guess you'll know when we get there, won't you?" Her eyes flash. My heart topples into my stomach not because of how breathtaking Blake's flashing eyes are but because her eyes are flashing at me and I want that. I want Blake to flash her eyes at me. To smile at me. To…

Bloody hell. I do have a crush on Blake. All this time I was never confused. I was just in denial. It's official then. I have feelings for two women, both of whom have zero romantic interest in me. *Well that's just fabulous. So. Fucking. Fabulous.*

Chapter Twenty-Three

Blake

I would like to think that I know what I'm doing as I turn the key to the door of my place. My heart is hammering so loud that it's alarming. I hope Hayden can't hear the uproar in my chest. She's standing about three feet behind me in complete silence. *Is she uncomfortable? Is this a bad idea?* Only one way to find out. I take an inconspicuous calming breath, pull my key from the lock, turn the knob and prod the door open. *Fuck. What am I doing?*

"Welcome," I say as I step inside my home.

Hayden doesn't say anything. I turn around and Hayden is loitering in the threshold. "Or you can stay there. That's cool too," I jest.

Hayden canvasses the area of my condo that's within her line of vision. "This is where you live?"

I raise an eyebrow at her, trying to curtail a smile. "What was the tip-off? It was the keys, wasn't it?"

Hayden pouts. "No, it's just that I...um...I didn't know that this is where you were going to take me. Like when we parked in the garage of this complex I thought...I don't know what I thought. I don't even know if I was thinking."

I purse my lips. "Do you want to leave?"

"No."

"Are you uncomfortable?"

Hayden half-shakes her head. "No but do you usually bring your friends to your apartment?"

"If you're referring to my *one* friend, then yes. Grace comes over often."

"Okay."

"Are you sure you're not uncomfortable?" I ask.

"I'm sure."

138

"Perhaps you'd like to come inside then?"

Hayden nods and shuffles through the entryway of my home. She closes the door behind her and takes in her surroundings. Once she's finished surveying my living quarters, she looks at me.

"You have a seriously nice apartment. The rent must be astronomical."

I shrug. "I don't pay rent. I own it." I make as if I can't see Hayden gaping at me and point to the liquor cabinet. "Can I get you a drink?"

"You own this?"

"Wine? Whiskey? Beer?"

Hayden smooths her hand over the marble island in my kitchen. "Whiskey."

I remove the bottle of whiskey from the cabinet and give it to Hayden. "Would you mind holding this?" I ask her. Hayden takes the bottle from me and I grab two clean glasses from the dish rack. "Now if you'll follow me," I say and lead Hayden over to the high-top table located in the middle of the dining area. If Hayden were some other woman, this is the part when I'd lure her into my bedroom. And even being fully aware that it IS Hayden here and not some other woman, there's still a part of me that wants to lure her into my bedroom. *Oh man. To see her in nothing but those suspenders...*I give myself a mental shake to clear my head. *Concentrate.* I place the glasses down on the table and sit. I motion to the empty chair across from me. "Have a seat."

Hayden sets the whiskey on the table and sits. I open the bottle and pour a small amount of alcohol into each glass. I slide a drink towards Hayden.

"Thank you," Hayden mumbles.

"I bought this place six months ago. I got a handsome bonus and made an investment."

139

"Wow. That's awesome. I feel confident that I'll be renting for the rest of my life."

"You never know." I take a sip of my drink.

"Why were you acting all modest about owning it?" I place my right hand over my heart. "What? You don't think I can be modest?"

Hayden snorts. "Not really."

"Well, I can be so…" I stick my tongue out at Hayden. For the first time since we left Adrianna's Pie House, Hayden smiles. I sigh. "Honestly though, I hate the look of shock on people's faces when I tell them that I'm a homeowner. They're so confounded by the idea that someone who doesn't have a college degree and works in retail full-time can pull off such an achievement."

Hayden furrows her brow. "Did I give you a shocked look?"

"Yep."

I watch as Hayden's ears redden. She cringes. "I'm sorry."

"It's cool. I'm used to it."

"Why don't you think of it as being a total bad-ass, breaking that societal stereotype instead?"

I smirk. "I do that every day being a lesbian who passes."

Hayden gasps. "Wait. You're a lesbian?"

I roll my eyes even though I am amused. "Har. Har." "That's so rad," Hayden continues. "Because I'm a lesbian too."

"Nooo." I breathe out. "You don't say."

"I do say." Hayden grins and takes a drink of whiskey. She waves one arm around as if presenting my dining room. "Your parents must be proud."

Ugh. Do I really want to go there? My memory quickly retrieves a comment Grace made about feeling sad for me and my refusal to make genuine connections. I grimace inwardly.

"If they are, they haven't told me," I say. "My parents and I are what you'd call 'distant'."

Hayden gives me a melancholic look. "Oh."

I force a smile. "Fix your face. It's fine."

"Can I ask you something?"

"Ask away."

"On Cyberjournal, there's a picture of you in front of a Christmas Tree with two people. Are they your parents?"

"They are."

"But you don't talk to them?"

I scoff. "I don't talk to them. They don't talk to me. It's whatever."

Hayden's frown deepens.

"Please don't feel sorry for me," I say.

"Are you going to tell me why?"

"I wasn't planning on it."

"Try," Hayden encourages.

I gape. "And you think *I'm* bossy?"

"Okay. You don't have to tell me."

I shut my eyes for a second. *Christ on a cracker.* I clear my throat. "That picture was taken when I was still in high school...dating Connor. Then I stopped dating Connor and came out to them. They weren't huge fans of the whole having-a-gay-daughter thing, so they gave me a choice: I go to conversion therapy or leave. I peaced out. I was seventeen. I went to a youth shelter—that was fun—and worked my ass off that year every day after school. As soon as I turned eighteen, I got my own apartment."

Hayden studies my expression, but I'm exceptionally good at masking my feelings especially my hurt.

"Thank you for sharing." Hayden speaks softly.

"Glad you asked?"

141

"I am actually."

Oh. "What about you? Your photos on Cyberjournal don't give much insight to your personal life."

"That's on purpose."

"I kind of figured," I say with a smirk.

"What do you want to know?"

What you look like underneath all those button down shirts. "Are you close with your parents?"

Hayden shifts in her seat. "No."

"Is this sharing thing one-sided because if it is, that's bogus."

Hayden polishes off her drink and studies the bottom of the empty glass for several seconds. "My parents don't talk to me either."

I can hear the pain in Hayden's voice. I want to reach over and take her hand, but I don't. "I'm sorry."

Hayden glances up at me wearing a sad smile. She waves her index finger back and forth. "Tut-tut. No feeling sorry."

I nod. "Right."

Hayden's perfect smile vanishes as quickly as it appeared. She turns the glass around in her hands and then balls her hands into fists. She swallows and shakes her head. I wait. Hayden exhales and levels her eyes to mine. Her blue gaze is misty. My chest clenches.

"Mom and Dad think that what happened to Evie is my fault; that our family falling apart is my fault. I don't blame them," Hayden says quietly.

"Who's Evie?" I hold my breath.

Hayden clears her throat and stares up at the ceiling. A tear escapes from the corner of her left eye and drifts down her cheek. I use all of my restraint and instead of wiping Hayden's tear away, I let it stain her skin.

"Evie was my sister."

Was. My stomach coils.

Hayden lowers her eyes to me. "It was my responsibility to watch over her. That's what a big sister does, but I messed up. I introduced her to Bryce on the night of my college graduation party. She begged me. She said he was a 'dreamboat'." Hayden cracks a small, wistful smile and rolls her eyes, but when she does, another tear falls. "I only knew Bryce because we had a few classes together. He always seemed friendly so I didn't see the harm. I never would have thought..." Hayden pauses as if the words she's trying to say are choking her. She clears her throat again. "Anyway, I introduced Evie to Bryce and Bryce introduced Evie to heroin."

Jesus. I go stiff in my seat. I don't need Hayden to tell me what happens next, but I think she wants me to know. So I don't say anything. I wait for Hayden to continue. After about a minute of soundlessly staring at one another, Hayden speaks.

"The following two years were a nightmare. Evie was in and out of rehabs. Sometimes she'd disappear altogether only to return weeks later to tell our parents about her newfound sobriety. Then within days, money would go missing from my dad's wallet or my mom would be missing some jewelry and Evie would be using again. The last time she dipped, she was gone for almost a month, but when she came back she swore she was clean. My mom believed her. My dad didn't. I wanted to, but I was leery. She was home for two full days and on day number three, I went to wake her up. It was her birthday. I was going to take her out for breakfast. My dad had taken the locks off of her doo,r so I just knocked and then walked in." Hayden shuts her eyes and tightens her jaw, but the tears she was trying to hold in flow freely anyway. A sorrowful ache stabs at my heart. Hayden opens her eyes.

They're bluer than usual; darkened by grief. "I found her. She was on the floor, slumped over like maybe she had been sitting with her back against the bed. Her right hand was still loosely holding onto the needle. I tried to wake her up. I shook her. I screamed at her. I yelled for my parents to call 911 while I attempted CPR even though I knew. I had to try." The edges of Hayden's mouth turn down. "She was dead. Evie was dead."

Hayden inhales sharply through her nose. "When the coroner's report came back, it said she died about an hour before I found her. I was one hour late." Hayden nods. "One hour. You know, I did the math. Evie died twenty-four minutes after she turned twenty-four. Weird, huh?" Hayden presses her lips together. "So, my parents never forgave me for introducing Evie to Bryce. The way they see it, Evie's addiction to heroin was my fault. And they couldn't deal. They were angry at me, angry at each other. Finally, they got divorced."

Fuck. That's a lot.

"Glad you asked?" Hayden's question is meant to be sarcastic, but I hear the inflection of fear in her voice.

This time, I do it. I reach over and I take Hayden's right hand between both of mine.

"Yeah. I am," I say. "Thank you for sharing." Hayden scoffs. I squeeze her hand in response.

"I'm so so sorry for all of your losses but none of that was your fault. You know that, right? It's not your fault."

"It is my fault," Hayden whispers.
Automatically, I get out of my seat. I maintain my grip on Hayden's hand as I round the table. Once I'm beside her, she looks up at me. I tug her hand, inviting her to stand. Hayden slowly rises to her feet. Now we're facing one another, holding hands.

Reflexively, I place my left palm against Hayden's right cheek. Her skin is so soft. "Listen to me. It's not your fault. I promise. Okay?"

Hayden's lower lip starts to tremble. "Okay." She lowers her forehead onto my shoulder and begins to cry.

I let go of Hayden's hand and wrap my arms around her.

"Okay. You're okay. I got you." The truth is though, it's Hayden who has me.

Chapter Twenty-Four

Hayden

I cannot believe I'm crying in front of Blake. Pull it together. I attempt to take a deep breath, but a small sob dislodges from my throat. I cringe on the inside. *Yikes. That sounded rough. Okay. Breathe. Slow and steady.* I exhale shakily without impersonating a dying animal. Good. I'm improving. However, when I inhale, I don't just inhale air. I inhale Blake. *God she smells amazing. Wait. Oh shit. We're hugging.* I lose the ability to breathe again as I lose myself in Blake's lilac-y scent. The overwhelming sadness that the memory of Evie's death had unleashed begins to lessen. *Inhale. Exhale.* Gradually, my breathing becomes controlled. I don't want to move though. I want to stay in Blake's arms. *That's normal, right? Because crushes.*

I open my eyes. Strands of Blake's silky brown hair tickle the side of my face. Her neck is dangerously close to my lips. *Keep all thoughts platonic.* I have to move. I pull away haltingly, giving myself enough time to inhale Blake's essence once more. Our cheeks brush and as a jolt charges down my spine, leaving my flesh covered in goosebumps, I hear Blake gasp. *Did she feel something too?* We're suddenly both very still, our mouths only inches apart. I can practically taste the whiskey on her breath. Every cell in my body is awake. A million thoughts flood my mind and none of them are platonic.

"You good?" Blake murmurs.

I swallow and answer softly, "Yeah. Better. Thanks."

Blake edges her face away from mine as she lets go of me. "Sure." She gives me a strained smile. "Can I get you another drink?" She takes a step backward creating at least two feet of space between us.

"Um. I should probably pass. I'm tired and we still have to get my car and then I have to drive home."

Blake glances at the clock on the wall and then at me. "It's late. You could stay here if you want."

What? I stare at Blake, wide-eyed. "What?"

Blake smirks. "You heard me. You're welcome to spend the night here. I'll take you to get your car in the morning. Or not. It's up to you."

Holy hell. An unexpected image of what Blake might look like in her unmentionables temporarily hijacks my thoughts. Heat blankets my body.

"I. Uh. I don't want to put you out," I manage.

Blake raises an eyebrow at me. "Hayden, you're not nervous are you?" There's a playful lilt in her voice.

Uh. Yeah I am. "Why would you ask me that?"

"Your ears."

"Awesome."

Blake chuckles. "Don't be embarrassed. I told you, it's endearing." She bites her bottom lip and tips her head to the side. She squints at me suspiciously. "Question is *why* are you nervous?"

Just come clean already. Get it over with. It'll hurt like fuck if you carry around these feelings the way you did with Ava and look at where that got you.

"Have you never spent the night at a woman's place without the nude scene?" Blake asks.

I clear my throat. "I've never spent the night at a woman's place. Period."

Blake gapes, but she's fast at closing her mouth. "Oh. Well okay then. I will get my keys and drive you back to your car." She turns to exit the room.

No. Don't. For a second, everything stops. I'm not thinking about Ava. I'm not grieving for Evie. It's just me and Blake.

I hastily reach out and arrest Blake by her left wrist. "No. Don't."

Chapter Twenty-Five

Blake

My heart stops. I steel myself, catch my breath and glance down at Hayden's fingers wrapped around my wrist. I slowly turn to face her and she releases me quickly.

"I'm sorry," Hayden blurts. "I just...I'll stay. I want to stay."

Great. Now I'm nervous. "Okay."

"I have to tell you something though."

Please be something about kittens or world peace. "Okay. What?"

Hayden digs the toe of her right sneaker into my hardwood floor. "You might not want me to stay after I tell you."

Wonderful. "Why don't you tell me and we'll find out?"

Hayden nods. "I think I'll take you up on that drink." *Ugh. This is not going to be good.*

"Sure." I take a step towards Hayden mostly because she's standing close to where the bottle of whiskey is resting on the table, but also because I want to be as near to her as possible. Before I reach for the bottle, I eye Hayden. "You know you don't need liquid courage to tell me anything," I say. "We're friends."

"About that." Hayden winces.

My stomach churns. "We're not friends?"

"No. No. No. We're friends. We're totally friends. That's not it."

"Then what is it?" *Does she like me the way I like her?*

"I don't know how to say this."

"Try."

"You're bossy." Hayden smiles.

"Grr. Quit it with the suspense. Tell me."

"I think you're attractive," Hayden utters suddenly.

I roll my eyes, but smile. "This again?"

"I know that you know that I think that because I told you but..."

"But what?" I urge.

Hayden swallows so hard I can see the muscles in her neck move. "It's more than that."

Say it. I boldly take another step towards Hayden. If I move any closer, our bodies will touch. "Say it." I unabashedly stare at her mouth. *That bottom lip.*

"I'm infatuated with you."

YESSS! "Oh yeah?"

"Yeah."

I raise my gaze and our eyes lock.

"Is that your fancy way of telling me you have a crush on me?" I ask.

"Maybe."

"Maybe or definitely?"

"Definitely." Hayden's voice is low and inviting. I want her.

"Does this mean you want to fuck me?"

Hayden's eyes widen and her brow creases. "What? I don't understand. What's going on here? What are you—"

I press my index finger against Hayden's lips. "Do you always ask this many questions when a woman's trying to seduce you?" I remove my finger from her mouth with a warning look. Hayden's breath hitches. *So hot.*

"I thought I wasn't your type."

"About that." I smirk. "Forget I ever said it."

Hayden's beautiful blue eyes narrow as she takes in my words. "Forgotten."

"Good. Now answer the question: do you want to fuck me?"

A hint of a grin plays on Hayden's lips. "Maybe."

I take hold of Hayden's suspenders and give them a light tug, pulling her in. There's no more space between us. "Maybe or definitely?" I whisper.

Unsmiling, Hayden whispers back, "Definitely."

"Then what are you waiting for?"

Chapter Twenty-Six

Hayden

Purely on instinct, I bring my left hand to the right side of Blake's face. I slide my fingers behind her ear and run my thumb along her cheek. Her lips slightly part. I tilt my head and lower my face to Blake's as I draw her to me. When our mouths are only a breath away, Blake closes her eyes and so do I. I brush my lips across Blake's. Her lips are softer than I imagined. I feel them on every inch of my body. My heart's beating wildly. I open my mouth a little to deepen the kiss. Blake doesn't hesitate. She slips her tongue into my mouth and circles my tongue with her own. My head's buzzing. I kiss her back harder. Our mouths quickly find their rhythm. My hand drifts from Blake's cheek to her neck, over her choker and onto her exposed shoulder. Her skin is smooth. I want to rip her shirt off. Blake captures my bottom lip between her teeth and pulls lightly. *My god.* When our lips connect again, she rakes the fingers of her right hand through my hair and grabs the back of my head. Our kiss becomes carnal. Needy. Blake releases me from her grip. Her hands fall onto my belt buckle. I lose my breath for a second.

"You're sure?" I gasp.

Blake unfastens my belt, her mouth hovers over mine.

"Yes," she rasps. "Are you?"

"Yes."

"Okay." Blake crushes her mouth against mine and untucks my shirt and the tank top beneath with one pull.

"I want you to know this isn't about anyone else," I murmur through our kiss.

"I know."

"I really do like you." My lips vibrate against Blake's.

"I like you too."

She does? I pull back a little further and stare at her. "You do?"

Blake licks her lips through a small exhale and meets my gaze. "Hayden."

"Yeah?"

Blake frees the button of my jeans. "I want to fuck you senseless."

Jesus she's sexy. I swallow and just keep staring at her.

"Will you let me?" Blake asks.

"Yes."

Blake gives me a coquettish smile. "Then stop talking and kiss me."

I reach up and take Blake's glasses off. I place them on the table. I take hold of the hem of her shirt and begin inching it upwards. Blake raises her arms and I pull the shirt over her head. Her top drops to the floor. My eyes automatically fall to Blake's chest. To the black, lace-trimmed demi bra she's wearing. To the way her wavy dark hair rests against her olive skin. She is more beautiful than any model in any picture. Ever.

I look her in the eyes once more. I put my hands on her bare hips and bring her closer. I kiss her collarbone. I feel her shiver. I run my tongue along her neck. She eagerly begins to unbutton my shirt starting from the bottom. I kiss her jawline. She tilts her face towards mine. Our noses graze. I sweep my lips across Blake's. She opens her mouth and kisses me hungrily as she loosens the last button on my shirt and slips her hands beneath my tank top. She presses her palms into my stomach then slides them up and over my breasts, my bra is still a barrier but it doesn't matter. *Her touch.*

I break our heated kiss and with a little force, I skillfully turn Blake to the side so that the front of her body is

153

facing the table. She lets out a small gasp and latches onto to the edge of the table. With one agile step, I'm behind her.

Chapter Twenty-Seven

Blake

I close my eyes when I feel the heat of Hayden's body against my backside. Her arms slip around my waist and I lean into her. I feel her ragged breaths on the back of neck. I tilt my head a little to the left. Instantly, her mouth is on my neck. I reach around with my left hand and grab Hayden by the back of her head as I crane my neck to the side. Hayden's mouth finds mine and we begin kissing with untamed urgency. Hayden's right hand tightens on my waist while she slides her other hand under my bra and squeezes my left breast with minimal pressure, but it's enough to elicit a small moan from my throat. I pull at her hair. Her fingers tease my nipple for a second. Pleasure ripples through my body. I push my ass further into her pelvis. Hayden pulls her left hand out from underneath my bra and she glides her fingertips down my side. It tickles and causes the tiny hairs on my arms to stand up. I run my tongue over Hayden's top lip as she expeditiously unfastens the button of my jeggings. She works the zipper of my pants and covers her mouth with mine. I let go of Hayden's hair and fervently assist her in pulling my jeans down over my hips. Hayden's hand smooths across my stomach then slinks beneath my black, satin thong. I feel my pulse everywhere. I tear my lips away from Hayden's to try to catch my breath but when she slides her two forefingers over my wet center, we both choke out a gasp and I'm left breathless again. Hayden begins rhythmically stroking my sex.

"Fuck." I exhale.

With one hand, Hayden gives my jeans another yank. She tugs at them until they're bunched up right below my knees. She locks me in another kiss as she begins to run her fingers steadily across my clitoris with magnificent precision.

My legs nearly give out. Heady with desire, I pull my mouth away from Hayden's. I grab her wrist to keep her hand in place and deftly turn around to face her. Our eyes meet for a moment and then her lips crash into my again. Her right hand grabs onto my outer thigh and I blindly grip the edge of the table behind me. In one fluid motion, we maneuver my body so that I'm sitting on the table all the while her fingers continue to work my clit. I wrap my arms around Hayden's neck as the tension in my body builds.

"There. Don't stop," I groan against Hayden's lips.

Hayden applies a bit more pressure and all of my muscles tense. "I'm right here," Hayden whispers and her voice sends a chill through me. My body convulses as ecstasy floods me. I arch my back suddenly and let out a low moan as I come against Hayden's fingers. *Oh my god.*

Hayden rests her forehead in the crook of my neck. Her lips skim my sweaty skin. I straighten up and hold her close. We're both panting. I bury my nose in Hayden's hair and relish the sweet smell of her shampoo. I kiss the side of her head and quietly say, "You might be my new favorite friend."

Chapter Twenty-Eight

Hayden

I lift my head from Blake's shoulder, kiss her jawline and press my forehead into hers.

"I *might* be your new favorite friend or I'm definitely your new favorite friend?" I tease.

Blake smirks. "My answer's pending."

"On?"

"What happens next." She kisses my nose and grabs onto my shoulder to balance herself as she hops off of the table and promptly removes her boots. She pulls her jeggings all the way down and discards them. Blake looks at me but I'm already staring at her, awestruck. She's only wearing her thong and that sexy bra I've imagined her in at least a million times. I take in every dip and curve of her figure and immediately ache to touch her again. Her cleavage is shiny with perspiration. Her sleek brown hair is slightly messy but in the sexiest of ways. I meet her gaze. The flecks of gold in her irises are especially noticeable and her eyes are sparkling at me. She is devastatingly gorgeous.

Blake takes ahold of the edges of my open button down. "See something you like?"

You don't even know. "Yes."

Blake licks her lips. "Me too." She steps away from the table. "C'mere." She starts walking backwards out of the dining room, pulling me by my shirt. We pass through the threshold and enter what appears to be the living room. When we reach the sofa, Blake's grip on my shirt tightens. She turns and takes me with her; redirecting me. She pushes me onto the couch. I slump against the cushions in a half-seated position. She places her left knee on the sofa between my legs and slowly seats herself on my left leg. *So hot. I can't even.*

Blake stares intently into my eyes. She carefully slips off my suspenders. "I'm all about these for the record."

"Noted."

Blake leans in and purposely drives her knee harder into my groin. She grinds her body against my leg. I can hear the blood racing through my veins. When her mouth is practically on top of mine, she runs her thumb across my bottom lip. She gently touches my lip ring. Then she moves her hand to my cheek and smooths a kiss over my lips. I open my mouth a little and Blake kisses me again. More forcefully this time. Her tongue massages mine as her body begins to move in time with our kiss. She takes off my shirts and tosses them aside. Her hands explore my naked skin. Her touch sends a chill through me. She breaks the kiss for a second and takes me in. She traces her index finger over the tattoo on my right bicep: an equality symbol within a heart. She bites her lower lip through a smirk. Suddenly her mouth is on mine again as her fingers continue traversing across my flesh.

"I'm so wet," Blake murmurs into my mouth.

I involuntarily moan and place my hand on Blake's upper thigh, inches from the edge of her panties. I want to feel how wet she is, but she seizes me by my wrist. Blake's lips start to travel down my neck, onto my shoulder, across my clavicle. She reaches behind me, unhooks my bra and greedily does away with it. Her mouth finds my breasts and one by one, she sucks on my nipples. I can't see straight. I close my eyes and lull my head back against the cushion. Blake slithers off of me as her tongue trails down my abdomen. She kisses my bellybutton. It tickles. I writhe from the sensation and open my eyes. I look down at Blake. She smiles an insanely sexy smile and winks at me. *This woman.* She continues to lower herself until she's on her knees between my legs. She grabs the waistband of my jeans. I lift myself just enough for her to wriggle my pants down. I hear the faintest laugh escape her between her uneven breaths.

"What's wrong?"

"Nothing." Blake lightly traces the fabric of my checkered boxer briefs with her fingertips. "You rock these."

"Thanks?"

Blake shakes her head. "You're fucking hot." Her head dips back down between my thighs. She kisses the inside of my knees and smooths her hands over the backs of my legs. She grips my calves as her tongue skids across the inside of my right thigh. I shut my eyes again. She kisses my center over my briefs. I jerk with excitement. Blake exhales heavily and tears off my underwear with abandon. Her fingernails dig into my calves and she sinks her teeth into my left thigh. After a few seconds, she kisses the spot where she deliberately meant to leave a mark. Then her tongue glides upwards and over my slick, swollen middle. We both draw in a loud breath. I pull at Blake's hair as she moves her tongue gracefully along my core. I lose my breath again. I lose my sense of space and time. I bite down on my bottom lip to stifle another moan when the tip of Blake's tongue grazes my clit. Then she begins to suck. A thrill rushes through me. Every nerve in my body responds to the feel of Blake. The movements of Blake's tongue become eager. I'm sweating. My heart slams rambunctiously against my chest as the pressure within me builds. Blake's tongue slows and begins to circle the source of my arousal for several seconds. Then she easily strokes my clit with her tongue in an up-and-down motion that makes my body buckle. All of my muscles tighten as Blake brings me closer to climax. Blake somehow manages to find my right hand and threads her fingers through mine. She squeezes my hand and a titillating sensation surges through me. I scratch at Blake's shoulders and spasm as I release.

I reach down and cup Blake's face within my hands. She peers up at me, smiling. Then she places her hands on the sofa on either side of me and pushes herself upward, off the rug. She settles into my lap and wipes her mouth with her right hand. She leans in and sweeps her lips across mine.

"Yeah," Blake says breathlessly. "You're definitely my new favorite friend."

Chapter Twenty-Nine

Blake

I groggily open my eyes and realize that my right leg is numb. It's sandwiched between Hayden's legs. The front of my body is curled up against her back side and seems to still be asleep. My right arm is draped over her waist. It rises and falls with her sleepy breaths. I smell her hair. We're sharing a pillow. We're beyond close—we're spooning...and we're naked. We're naked-spooning. *Shit.* Sex is one thing, but spooning? Spooning is a thing that couples do and Hayden and I are not a couple.

The alarm on my phone sounds, rescuing me from my spiraling thoughts about couplehood and self-preservation. *Work. I have to get up for work.* The alarm doesn't rouse Hayden. I carefully move my arm from Hayden's waist and roll over. Even then she doesn't stir. *Someone's a deep sleeper.* I pick up my phone from the bedside table and dismiss the alarm. Another bout of silence fills my bedroom. I return the phone to the table and look at Hayden; the shape of her beneath the covers. I bring my right hand up to my nose and inhale Hayden's scent from my fingertips. *God.* I smile but then I catch myself smiling and shake my head. *Get a grip. You have places to go and things to do.* I sigh knowing that I cannot keep this moment. I have to wake her up.

I sit up and slip the sheets off myself. I shift my body back towards Hayden's and lean down. My mouth lingers by her left ear for a second too long so that I can breathe in her morning smell again. *I am so pathetic.*

I kiss Hayden's earlobe lightly. She flinches and a slumberous smile tugs at the corners of her mouth.

"Hey," I whisper.

Hayden's eyes remain closed. "Hi."

"Time to get up."

"Why? What time is it?"

"It's early but I have to drive you back to your car and I have to go to work."

Hayden slowly opens her eyes and she squints up at me. She grins. "How do you feel about morning sex?"

I try not to smile. "I strongly support it, but we have to get going. You need to get dressed and I have to shower."

Hayden's eyebrows arch suggestively. "Do you want company?"

"Hayden!" I chide through a half-repressed chuckle.

Hayden laughs. "Alright. Alright." She reaches behind herself and tangles her fingers in my hair. She pulls me in for a kiss before I have time to protest or think or breathe. We both taste like morning but neither of us seems to care as our mouths become reacquainted. After a minute...or five, our lips languidly part.

"Good morning," Hayden says softly.

My chest warms and expands. *I'm in even more trouble than I thought.* "Good morning. Now get your sexy ass out of bed."

"Okay. I will, but can I see you again tonight? When you get out of work?"

Oh boy. "It'll be late."

"I don't care."

I blink deliberately and take one of Hayden's hands in mine. "I don't think that's a good idea."

"Why not?"

"Because we're friends."

Hayden's expression scrunches up. "Eh. I'd say we're a little more than friends."

"Fine. We're friends who had sex, but we can't make this a regular thing."

"Would it be so bad if it were a regular thing?" Hayden asks.

Yes because I like you WAY more than you like me and you're in love with your freaking best friend. "It could get messy. I don't think our friendship is worth the risk."

"What part of life isn't messy?" Hayden turns onto her back to better see me. She stares at me intently. "What if we make sex part of our friendship? Liiike we'll be special friends."

I shoot Hayden a stony-faced sardonic look. "You mean fuck buddies?"

"Or that."

I purse my lips and nod. "And what happens when your little crush on me turns into something much more and you fall in love with me?"

Hayden scoffs. "Please."

Okay. Ouch. "Gee. Thanks."

"Blake, come on. We both know you're completely fall-in-love-able, but my crush on you is just a crush and you don't do relationships, so we really can't be anything more than fuck buddies anyways. This could work. It's fail-safe."

Except that it's not because I already like you much more than either one of us wants me to.

"I won't have to prowl Luscious anymore. You won't have to log onto your dating apps," Hayden continues. "We'll have each other. We'll meet each other's sexual needs and—bonus—we're friends so there won't ever be any hard feelings. No one can get hurt. It's perfect."

"Most of the time, perfection is an illusion." Hayden frowns.

I shrug. "I told you. I'm a realist."

Hayden covers my hand with her other hand. "Perhaps perfection is in the eyes of the beholder."

I raise my eyebrows. "I told you, I'm a visionary."

Hayden chews on her bottom lip briefly. "And I'm kind of envisioning us having a whole lot of hot sex."

Aand I'm done. I totally lost that argument with Hayden and with myself because of course the best sex of my life had to be with her–the only woman whose heart I can never have. Awesome. The warning alarm on my phone goes off. I groan.

"I really have to go," I say.

"I know, but will you think about it?"

Ahahaha. Will I think about having sex with you? Um. Yes. Most definitely. I pull my hand from Hayden's hold, reach over to the bedside table and silence the alarm. I turn back to face Hayden. "Up. Up. Up. Let's go," I say.

"It's just sex."

"I think your clothes are still in the living room." I begin to get off the bed.

Hayden catches me by my forearm. "Are you mad?"

I sigh. "No."

"Then what's the matter?"

Everything. "Nothing."

"Was last night not good for you?"

I snort. "You were there. I think you know the answer."

"Then what's the problem?"

I know these kinds of things usually end badly. I've seen the movie. I've read the book. I've heard the song. But here we are, and Hayden is looking at me with her crystal blue eyes and I am entranced because if perfection does exist, it's in the way she kisses me and touches me. It's in her eyes. I hope I don't regret this. "I'll think about it." *Please don't let me regret this.*

164

Chapter Thirty

Hayden

It's not until I reach my apartment door after my short-lived morning with Blake that I begin to come out of a giddy stupor and think about Ava and our last interaction. Suddenly dread fills me. I can hear music coming from inside the apartment, which means Ava's home. I feel queasy as I turn my key in the lock and cautiously enter the apartment. Ava is right there in the kitchen by the sink. She finishes rinsing out a coffee mug and places it in the drying rack. I close the door behind me. Ava shuts the faucet off and turns to me. She looks me up and down questioningly.

"Hi," I say.

"Hi."

I gesture to her. "You're here."

Ava narrows her gaze at me. "I do live here."

I heedfully step further into the apartment, towards the kitchen entryway. "Obviously, but last night you made it seem like you were unsure about us being roommates."

"Yeah." Ava sighs. "We both said a lot of things last night."

My stomach lurches. I'm wishing right about now that I hadn't stopped to get a bagel and coffee on the way home because I really don't want to see my breakfast in reverse. I concentrate on taking a deep breath. *Inhale through the nose. Exhale through the mouth.*

"Yes. We did," I agree.

"Listen, Hayden, I've been thinking and I over-reacted. I'm sorry."

What? "What? No you didn't. You had every right to be upset with me. I shouldn't have kept all that from you. I just thought that if I told you that I had feelings for you then…I don't know. I didn't want to lose you or scare you or make things uncomfortable between us so I kept it to myself. I'm sorry."

Ava crosses her arms over her chest. "I get that. Sort of. It's just weird that you decided to tell me when you did because you had an iota of hope that I'd admit to the same romantic feelings you had and we could be together. Where is the sense in that?"

There is none. I hang my head in shame. "I'm sorry. It was foolish of me and I have no honorable excuse."

Ava presses her lips together tightly and nods. "Did you mean it when you told me that our whole friendship hasn't been a sham? That you stuck around in my life because you love me as a person and not because you were hoping all these years that I'd someday realize I was attracted to women and that you'd be among those women?"

"Of course I meant that. Nothing has been a sham. Our entire friendship has been the real deal." I swallow. "Aves, you're my best friend. You're the only family I have. I love you because you're so great. It doesn't matter to me whether you're gay or straight or bisexual or bicurious or anything, I'd still love you." *Inhale through the nose. Exhale through the mouth.* "Am I attracted to you? Yes. Did I think it would be awesome if you realized you were attracted to me? Yes. Did I handle all of this in the worst way ever? Absolutely. But the bottom line for me is that I still don't want to lose you."

"You didn't lose me," Ava says. "I love you…in a strictly platonic way, but this could get crazy awkward, you know? I really like the woman I've been seeing, and I'd want to be able to invite her over without worrying about your feelings. I care about you and I don't want to be the person who breaks your heart."

Everything inside of me comes to a still not because I'm heartbroken but because I'm not heartbroken and I should be. Shouldn't I be? Why am I not heartbroken? This is the scene when I'm forced to face the reality of my unrequited love for Ava, who is dating someone who is not me. I should be a wreck. What is wrong with me? Am I more emotionally stunted than I initially thought? *Oh god. Don't panic. It's alright. You're alright. Just keep breathing.* I force a blithe smile. "There's no need for you to concern yourself with my heart."

Ava's eyes widen. "So it won't bother you if I bring another woman home?"

It should but...but what? Aargh! What is wrong with me?! I purse my lips and shake my head. "It's your home as much as it is mine. You can bring over whomever you choose."

Ava tips her head to the side. "You're sure you wouldn't have an issue with that?"

I twitch in a half-nod-half-shrug; a shrod if you will. "Mmhmm." I motion towards the direction of my bedroom. "I'm glad we had this chat and I'm so glad that there's no bad blood between us. I think we should both try to move past this now and act as if it never happened. Don't you think?"

Ava frowns. "You're hurt."

Only I'm not. "Nah. I'll be fine."

"Do you want to talk more about it?"

"No. I'd really rather never talk about it again if that's alright with you."

Ava nods slowly. "Okay." She's still eyeing me very closely. "You're wearing the same outfit you had on last night," She observes.

Please, ears, do not blush. "It was a long night."

"So you do sleepovers now?"

I puff out a breath. "Um. I don't know. It kind of just happened."

There's a knowing glint in Ava's blue eyes that makes me want to bolt from what I strongly believe is an oncoming interrogation. "I thought you were going to hang out with Blake last night?" Ava asks.

I muss my own hair and clear my throat. My ears are on full burn mode. "Yeah. We did hang out."

Ava squints. "Uh huh. And you spent the night with her? With Blake?"

"It was late. I was tired. She was tired."

"Riiight."

I grit my teeth. "What? Please say whatever it is I know you want to say."

"Nothing. I thought you two were *just* friends and that you definitely didn't have a crush on her because that would be preposterous." Ava's voice is oozing with sarcasm.

"We are just friends. I told you...we were tired."

"Tired. Okay. So did you two get tired before or after you spent the whole night getting it on?"

I chuckle. "'Getting it on?' Aves, really?"

"You're not answering my question."

I gasp animatedly. "Are you insinuating that Blake and I had sex?"

"Ha! I'm not insinuating anything. I'm straight up asking you if you and Blake had sex."

"A lady never tells."

Ava bursts into laughter. "A lady also never comes home in the same clothes she wore the night before with sex hair."

I pout. "Leave my hair out of this."

Ava momentarily rubs her temples. She looks at me. "Dude, I'm trying to understand." Her brow furrows. "You declared your love for me, your best friend, and then you went out and slept with your only other friend, who you have a crush on? You do realize how complicated you're making your own life, right? Are you trying to self-sabotage?"

"I never said I had sex with Blake or that I have a crush on her." *Even though I absolutely had the best sex of my life with her and am one thousand percent crushing on her.*

"And I will never believe that."

I stick my tongue out at Ava. "Besides it's not complicated. You're both still my friends. You don't have romantic feelings for me and neither does she."

"Are you sure that she doesn't have a crush on you?"

"Yes."

"What makes you so sure?"

"She's a player," I say. "Players don't get crushes."

Ava raises her eyebrows at me. "*You're* a player."

I furrow my brow. "Your point?"

"You have a crush ergo players can have crushes."

"Pfft. Even if I did have a crush, it would be fleeting." *I'm certain it's fleeting.*

"Is that right?"

"That is right."

Ava purses her lips. "Does she know about Evie?"

I swallow. "Yes."

Ava sighs. "Hayden, that's serious. You're letting her in. You wouldn't be making a connection with her if you thought she was just passing through."

I know. I open my mouth but nothing comes out. *I'm now extremely uncertain that this crush is fleeting. Welp this all escalated quickly from uncomplicated to extraordinarily sucky.*

"It's okay." Ava reaches out and pets my bicep. "Let it marinate."

"Marinating," I mumble.

"It's time for you to listen more closely."

169

"To what?"

"The sound of your heart, dummy" Ava says. "You think it's beating for me...and maybe it is." Ava pauses. "Or maybe it's not. That's something only you can figure out."

I don't actually see Ava walk away but her words reverberate between my ears.

Chapter Thirty-One

Blake

I take the last sip of my iced quad espresso and throw the cup in the trash bin next to my desk. My lunch break is almost over. I pick my cell phone up from my desk and stare at the Tap That app icon on the screen. I can't bring myself to open the app. I toss my head back theatrically and groan. I refocus on my phone's screen and open my saved contact list. I find Hayden's name.

"What am I going to do with you?" I mutter. "You're driving me crazy."

There's an unexpected knock on my office door. I immediately shove my phone in the waistband of my leggings. "Come in," I call out.

I watch the door slowly open and Julie pops only her head inside. She looks around my small office curiously and then at me.

"Hi." Julie draws out her greeting.

"Hey."

"Um. Are you busy? I heard you talking."

That's because I was talking to a name on my phone...you know, like a completely sane person.

"No. I'm not busy. I was about to come back out on the floor. What's up?"

"I came to tell you that someone's here asking for you."

An influx of butterflies flutter through my belly.

"Did they say who they were or what they wanted?" I ask in feigned nonchalance.

"It's that woman," Julie drops her voice. "The cute one who could rock the boxer briefs."

171

My heart ricochets against my ribcage. *You mean the cute one who DOES rock the boxer briefs.* "Oh. Okay. Just tell her I'll be out in a sec...please."

Julie tries to suppress a smile. "Sure."

"Thanks."

Julie nods and as her head disappears from the sight, the door shuts. I walk over to my locker and place my phone inside. I smooth my hands over my beige sweater and brace myself.

Just be cool. She's your friend. Nothing's changed. Except that's a lie. Everything has changed.

I exit my office and casually make my way through the store while furtively looking for Hayden. I spot her standing by the perfume display seemingly reading the label on one particular bottle. Right as I'm about to approach her, she glances up and catches sight of me. She smiles. *Ugh. That smile.* I smile back at her.

Hayden gives me a shameless once-over and her smile turns into a grin. "Hey, you," she says.

"Hi."

"Is it alright that I came to visit you at your work?"

"It depends. What's the reason for your visit?"

"I was wondering if my friend wanted to grab lunch with me."

"Ahh. I see."

Hayden's ears blush. "Um. You'd be the friend I'm referring to."

I chuckle softly. "I got that."

"Right. So..." Hayden gestures to the doorway of Undercover, her unfinished question lingering in the air.

I wince. "I already took my break."

Hayden frowns. "Oh. Well maybe some other time."

"Maybe."

Hayden raises the perfume bottle she's been holding in her right hand. "Is this what you wear? It smells like you."

I glimpse at the bottle of Pixie Dust then fix my eyes on Hayden. "It is."

"It smells great on you."

A memory of Hayden's naked body scaling my own, kissing me, breathing in my skin–my scent– storms through me. I instantly want to tear off her tapered leg chinos and pullover sweatshirt and fuck her in the dressing room. *Get ahold of yourself.*

I clear my throat. "Thanks."

Hayden nods as she places the bottle back in its rightful home on the display shelf. She faces me. "I came here Friday afternoon before our…meet up," she admits. "You weren't here."

"So you went shopping?"

Hayden's eyes narrow speculatively at me. "How did you…"

"You rock the briefs." I wink. "Like really really."

Hayden's cheeks rouge. "Wow. You know your product well."

"That's what they pay me for."

"Right and you…you um…look nice in…" Hayden's voice trails and she moves her left hand up and down in front of me as if she's showcasing me. "Everything."

"You haven't seen me in everything yet." I smirk.

Hayden quirks an eyebrow at me. "Yet?"

I chuckle. "Go home, Hayden."

"You don't mean that."

"I do actually because I've got things to take care of before my shift is over."

"But I'll hear from you?"

"I should be home by 11:30."

"Is that an invitation?"

I shrug and smile coyly.

Hayden purses her lips and points at me, but doesn't say anything. We stare at each other silently for a moment, both of us waiting for something more from the other but neither of us cracks. Eventually, Hayden shakes her head but her eyes are smiling. "Good day then," Hayden says and turns away from me. I don't stop her from leaving but I'm sure to admire her backside as she goes.

See you later, Cutie, I think to myself.

"What are you grinning about?" Kendall's voice startles me from behind.

I was grinning? Gross. Stupid crush. I gape. "What? I wasn't grinning."

Kendall laughs a little and as she passes me on her way to the registers she quietly says, "You were totally grinning."

Chapter Thirty-Two

Hayden

I'm standing outside of Blake's condo by 11:28 p.m. I lift my right fist to knock, but hold it still in the air. *What if I'm misreading this whole situation and I end up making a fool out of myself?* I take a breath. *Stop overthinking.* I nod to myself and knock on Blake's door. As I wait for her to answer, my grip tightens on the paper bag of Thai food in my left hand. After a couple seconds, Blake opens the door a crack. I can only see her face. She looks me up and down.

"I didn't order any food," she says, stone-faced.

"I thought you might be hungry after a long shift."

Blake smiles a little. "Thanks for coming over."

"Thanks for inviting me."

Blake inches the door open until her body is in full view. She's poised in the doorframe wearing only a white blouse and black mesh hipster thongs fastened to a pair of matching mesh black thigh highs. My heart does a cartwheel. Or six.

"Do you want to come in?" Blake asks smoothly.

Yes! So much yes! "Ask me a real question."

Blake grabs the strings of my hoodie and uses them to pull me inside. As soon as I'm inside, she shoves me against the door, the force of my body shutting it. I lose my breath to the element of surprise. Blake presses herself into me, our mouths daringly close to one another's. Her eyes are fixed on mine and she doesn't look away as she takes the bag of food from my hand and places it on a small table to our right.

"Too aggressive?" Blake murmurs.

I swallow. "No."

"Good." Her fingers play along the waistband of my chinos. "Then can I lick your pussy?"

Please do. I half smile. "Still not a real question."

Blake kisses my top lip. "Still gonna wait for answer."

If she were any sexier I'm sure I'd be dead. "The answer is yes."

"Good." Blake masterfully unfastens my pants in one swift motion. She kisses me longingly. I close my eyes. At once, I'm lost in the warmth of her mouth, the rhythm of our tongues tasting each other. Her right hand slinks beneath my boy briefs. She runs her index and middle fingers over my center. I shut my eyes tighter and revel in her touch. *I'm dead.*

I'm uncertain about how much time has passed between the moment I arrived at Blake's tonight and this moment right now. Blake and I are lying naked on the sofa facing each other. We're both breathless, recovering from the multiple orgasms we gave one another. We're both sweaty. And we're both smiling tiredly.

Blake nods. "Well, that was…intense."

I let out a soft chuckle. "Good intense or bad intense?"

"Good intense."

"Good."

"I definitely need to refuel now though." Blake glances behind herself at the paper bag on the table by the door. "What kind of food did you bring?"

"Thai. Green curry."

"Nice."

"Are you hungry?"

I can feel the growl forming in the pit of my stomach. "Yes."

"Let's feast then." Blake gets up from the sofa and rummages through the pile of our clothes on the floor. She finds her underwear and slips them on. Then she lifts my hoodie off the floor. She holds it up to me. "Do you mind?"

I furrow my brow. "Do I mind what?"

Blake pulls the sweatshirt over her head and pushes her arms through the sleeves. Her long hair splays over the hood. She grins at me. "So? Do you mind?" Blake asks again.

No. I positively do not mind. Blake looks ridiculously sexy in nothing but my hoodie and her thong. I'm already planning on not washing that hoodie so that I can smell her smell on it long after we part ways. "Nope." I shake my head as I answer.

Blake smiles at me. "It's cozy."

"I know. That's why it's my favorite."

"If it's your favorite then I'll be sure to keep it safe."

"I appreciate that."

"Of course." Blake winks and waltzes towards the door and I dutifully delight in her backside and bare legs as she does. She retrieves the bag of food and brings it back to where I'm at on the sofa. I sit up, pick my undershirt and boy briefs up off the floor, and quickly put them on. Once I'm half-dressed, I situate myself on the far right cushion.

"How do you feel about cold green curry?" Blake inquires.

"I feel good about it."

"Awesome." Blake takes a seat on the middle cushion of the couch and places the bag between us. She opens it up and inhales deeply. "Ah! This smells delish!" She takes out one of the two containers of food in the bag and hands it to me along with a pair of chopsticks.

"Thank you." I separate my chopsticks, open the container and poke at the food.

"Thank YOU for bringing me dinner."

"Even though you didn't order food?" I retort.

Blake snickers. "Even though I didn't order food. Yes."

"You're welcome."

Blake takes a bite of her green curry. "Mmm. So delish."

I begin eating my food and nod in agreement.

"Do you want something to drink?"

"Um. No. I'm okay right now." I look around the living room. "What time is it even?"

Blake purses her lips and then reaches to the floor. She feels around for a second and then grabs her phone. She peers at the screen. "The current time is 2:27 a.m."

"Oh. Wow. That's late."

"Technically, it's early." Blake smirks before taking another bite of food.

I stick my tongue out at her. "You know what I mean."

"I do know what you mean." Blake squints at me in the dimly lit room. "Why? Do you have to go?"

"No. It's just that I'm usually sleeping at this time."

"Well, you can sleep here if you want."

I try to hide my smile by eating another mouthful of food. "I might take you up on that."

"You should take me up on that."

"But I'll get heartburn if I try to sleep right after I eat."

Blake laughs. "What are you, ninety years old?"

"What? Why are you making fun of me? Anyone at any age can get heartburn."

"Mmhmm." Blake is still laughing.

"They can!" I proclaim as I start to laugh too.

"Then we won't lay down when we're done eating."

I bite my bottom lip. "We won't? Then whatever will we do?"

"Now. Now, Ms. Walcott. Calm that dirty mind of yours." Blake rests her chopsticks inside the container. She shrugs. "We could talk."

I inwardly wince at the intimate suggestion because I know that if I get any closer to Blake in any way than I already am, my crush on her will only magnify. Then I'll end up becoming one of those girls people write about who ends up having a major case of the feels for her fuck buddy. And I can't do the unrequited feels thing again. I cannot end up being that girl.

I swallow my food and look at Blake. There's a light from outside that's peeking through her miniblinds and it makes her eyes appear extra sparkly.

"Sure. We can talk." *Stellar job resisting intimacy, self.*

Chapter Thirty-Three

Blake

We could talk?! Why in the hell did I suggest that?
Why the hell did she agree? I'm so fucked. Ugh. Fuck my life.
"Cool. So let's talk," I say giving nonchalance my best shot. "How are things going with Ava?"

Hayden coughs then puts her food down.

"Good. Our friendship is still intact."

Hayden places her half-eaten dinner in the paper bag and glances at me. She forces a smile and looks away, giving the paper bag between us her full attention.

"It's funny that you brought up Ava," Hayden starts.

I cock my head to the side curiously. "Why's that?"

"She said something to me earlier and it was weird."

I stare at Hayden. "What did she say?"

"She alluded to the idea that possibly I was not in love with her; that I only think I am...or was...or..." Hayden shakes her head. "Never mind."

Was? Huh. I nod and put my food container in the bag on top of Hayden's.

"Why would she say that?" I ask.

Hayden runs her hand through her hair. "I don't have a clue."

Such a bad liar. "I call your bluff," I say.

Hayden smiles and steals another glimpse of me before her eyes are on that bag again.

"What makes you think I'm bluffing?"

I grab the paper bag and place it on the floor. Now there's just a few inches of empty space between us.

"Because you're avoiding eye contact," I say. "You're an easy read."

Hayden chuckles under her breath. "Ava says that about me all the time."

"There you have it."

"Yeah," Hayden mutters.

"Hayden, what's up? What is it that you're not telling me?"

"Aargh." Hayden shakes her head and finally looks at me with a steady gaze. "Ava knows that I...she knows about my crush on you."

I secretly pride myself at the fact that Hayden talks about me to her best friend.

"Okay. And?"

"This is dumb."

"What's dumb?"

"Ava thinks that because I have a crush on you and told you about..." Hayden's shoulders jerk and she presses her lips together.

This has to be about Evie. My chest aches a little watching Hayden struggle to say her sister's name. I rest my left hand gently on her right hand, but I don't speak.

"Ava thinks that because I told you about Evie, I'm letting myself connect with you...like in a special way."
The tips of Hayden's ears redden.

Wait. What kind of a special way?

"Oh." I manage to respond while simultaneously managing to successfully sound like a complete idiot.
Awesome. "Special in what way?"

Hayden turns her hand beneath mine and touches my fingers. She shrugs with her mouth. "Hell if I know."

Christ. Just ask her.

"Are you still in love with Ava?" It takes me a second to realize I'm holding my breath. Hayden stares thoughtfully at our pile of clothes on the floor and then turns to face me again.

"I always thought that what I felt for Ava was love. I'd never been in love before I met her and I'd feel things around her that I didn't feel around other women so I just figured it was love. I feel safe with her and she accepts me and she's crazy good-looking...how could that not be what in love is?" Love isn't exactly where my expertise is at. Now sex...sex is a completely different matter. The only thing I know for sure about love is that it's an uncontrollable force that can hurt you.

"Is that a hypothetical question?" I'm desperately trying to bide time here.

"No. I really want to hear your thoughts."

I wince. "Um. I'm not good at love."

"That can't be entirely true because you've been in love, right? With Sarah? You must have some thoughts about it."

Sarah. Ugh. I let out a slow exhale in attempt to alleviate the oncoming nausea courtesy of the memory that is Sarah.

"Yeah," I drawl. "Sarah."

Hayden frowns. "Sorry. I shouldn't have brought her up."

I wave away Hayden's apology. "You're fine." I purse my lips. "Okay. You're right. I suppose I have some thoughts about love."

"Blake, you don't have to share if it's too hard."

I sniff out a light laugh. "Sharing is never easy for me, but I'll give it a go...because we're friends and all." The word 'friends' leaves a sour taste in my mouth. I sigh dramatically to ease my own tension. "Alright. Here's what I think about love: you'll never see it coming but you'll know when it's arrived; when you're in it. It's complex and chaotic and painfully exquisite. It can breathe life into nothingness and it can break you in ways you never thought possible. You can't fight it because it's an undefeatable force. Eventually, it will get the best of you and the result of that could be amazing or unbearable. And if you have to ask yourself if you're in it or not, you're not." I swallow and tighten my jaw. "That's what I think about love."

Hayden's staring at me wide-eyed. "Wow."

"Should I have sugar-coated that for you?"

Hayden shakes her head. "No. Absolutely not."

"I also think that everyone's experience of being in love is different so it's not my place to tell you what it is or isn't that you're feeling. That's something only you can do."

Hayden nods. "Thank you for sharing."

"You're welcome."

"Blake?"

"Yes?"

"Do you ever get tired?"

"Of?"

"Trying to protect your heart?"

Only until I met you. "That's my secret to keep."

"Okay. I respect that."

I stand up from the sofa and place my hand on Hayden's shoulder. "I'm going to bed. You coming?"

Hayden looks up at me and places her hand over mine. She grins. "Am I coming?" She chuckles. "With you, always."

I know Hayden's joking with her sexual innuendo so I smile, but I silently want her to mean what she said in all the ways in which it could be meant.

Chapter Thirty-Four

Hayden

I slowly open my eyes after a brief, but deep sleep. It takes about a minute for my vision to adjust to the darkness of Blake's bedroom. I sit up a little and glance at the clock on the small table by Blake's side of the bed. It's a little before six o' clock in the morning. I'm not sure what time Blake's alarm is set for but I'm sure it's set given the fact that she has to work today. I could go try to fall back asleep or...

I shift my weight so that I'm fully facing Blake, who's seemingly sound asleep. I prop myself up by nestling my bent elbow into the plush pillow and resting my head on my hand. Blake is apparently a side-sleeper. The right side of her body is sunken into the mattress. The right side of her face is mostly buried in her pillow. Her mouth is the tiniest bit open, which makes me smile a goofy smile to myself. *I'm such a jackass.* With each of Blake's shallow inhales and exhales, I become familiar with her sleepy breathing. It's quieter than a snore but she isn't an entirely silent sleeper either. I watch her left shoulder rise and fall along with her breaths for a few seconds before I pull the sheet up over her bare skin and brush a panel of her chocolate brown hair off of her neck. She doesn't move. Not even a little. A part of me wishes she'd wake up if for no other reason than I'd be able to look into her beautiful cognac-colored eyes. The other part of me is more than content studying how such a guarded human in a woken state can be so completely vulnerable whilst sleeping. Clearly the latter puts me nicely in the bona fide creeper category. I should wake her before she wakes up on her own and I totally freak her out, and I will, but not quite yet. Right now I'm watching, looking, marveling.

An unexpected warmth surges through my chest and I gasp a little. My heartbeat quickens and my stomach begins doing acrobatics. This is hardly the first time I've experienced a physical reaction to Blake, but something about this feels different; more absolute in nature. I don't know what this is but I also somehow know exactly what this is.

I open my mouth to silently say the words just to see how they taste, but right as I'm about to speak, Blake begins to rouse. Her eyelids flicker open and she gives me a lazy smile.

"Good morning," Blake greets me and then yawns.

"Good morning."

"Were you watching me sleep?"

"It's possible that I watched you for like a second."

Blake smirks. "Riiight."

"What?"

"Creep."

I chuckle a little. "You're pretty when you're sleeping."

Blake narrows her eyes at me. "And what am I when I'm awake? Hideous?"

I wince. "No. That's not what I meant."

"I'm kidding, Hayden. Relax."

I rest my hand on Blake's hip. "When you're awake, you're dazzling."

"Ah. I bet you say that to all the girls you fuck."

"No. Only you."

Blake reached over and touches my cheek. "Aren't you sweet?"

"Actually, no. I'm horny as fuck and just trying to warm you up to morning sex."

Blake laughs. "Consider me warmed."

I raise an eyebrow. "Yeah?"

"Well, I'm sure my breath is kicking like whoa, so you can use your best judgement."

"Mine's probably worse."

"I'll take my chances."

I grin. "As will I."

Blake's hand slides from my cheek to the back of my head and she lures me closer. Our lips meet without hesitation. I pull the sheet off of us and climb on top of her. I break our kiss for a moment. "How much time do you have?" I ask.

"How much time do you need?"

I kiss her chin. "Enough to make you come in my mouth."

Blake grins. "You're good. I'm not worried."

I nod slowly, my face closing in on Blake's again. We resume kissing. I'm immediately intoxicated by the feel of Blake's tongue skimming across mine; by the taste of her; the smell of her. In all my life to date, this is by far my most favorite morning.

Chapter Thirty-Five

Blake

"Somebody's glowing." Grace grins maniacally as she takes her seat across from me at our table at The Bean.

"It's been a good week," I say matter-of-factly.

"It's only Tuesday, dude."

"I'm aware...and like I said, the week's been hella good thus far."

Grace snorts. "*Hella* good, huh?"

"Yup."

"Oh yeah? Lots of sex?"

I bite down on the straw in my iced quad espresso and bear my teeth in an almost smirk.

"I'll take that as an affirmation," Grace says. "So the friends with benefits thing is working out with Hayden?"

"It really is the best sex I've ever had."

Grace gives me a thumbs up as she takes a sip of her coffee. Then she clears her throat. "Have you told her?" Grace asks.

My brow furrows. "Have I told who what?"

Grace frowns. "Have you told Hayden how much you like her?"

"Umm. No."

"Blake! What the eff are you waiting for? Seriously."

I shrug. "What Hayden and I have is really great, you know? I don't want to ruin it with feelings and shit."

Grace quirks an eyebrow at me and shakes her head. "You idiot. 'Feelings and shit' are what you need to be sharing. You just said that what you two have is great. This is how you make it better. This is how you make it grow into something bigger. Tell her that you want to be more than vffs."

More than what now? My face scrunches up, confused. "What's a 'vff'?"

"Vagina Friends Forever. Der."

I blow out a short laugh. "Clever."

"I try." Grace wags her index finger at me. "Don't sidetrack me. I will not be sidetracked."

"Me? I would never sidetrack you."

"You're totally trying to sidetrack me right now."

I sigh. "What if I tell her and she dips? Not everyone is a fan of the feels."

"True. It's always risky to express to someone how you feel about them but eventually you're going to have to decide for yourself whether that's a chance you want to take or not. Personally, I think you should because if you don't, you may regret it forever and forever is a very, very long time. Like vampire lifespan long time."

I roll my eyes. Grace folds her hands on the table. "When are you seeing her again?"

Hopefully today. "I'm not sure."

"So today?" Grace gives me the side eye. "When you see her, tell her and let everything fall into place."

"And what if everything doesn't fall into place? What if everything falls apart?"

"Dude, have some faith."

"I'm a realist. Faith isn't exactly my thing."

"Mhmm. Right. And up until a few weeks ago, Hayden wasn't exactly your thing either. Things change. People change. Feelings change. It's all constantly flowing. Don't fight the flow."

The woman has a point. "Fuck you and your flow."

Grace gives me the finger. "Twat."

"Slutbag."

Grace snickers. "Fine. Do what you want but I need to ask you for a favor."

"Ugh. What?"

"I'm ready."

I tilt my head quizzically. "Ready for what?"

"I'm ready for you to meet the woman I'm dating."

I gasp and place my hand over my heart. "No way."

"Yes way."

"This is big," I say.

"It's astronomical." Grace smiles. "So are you in?"

"Of course I'm in!"

"Awesome. Can you meet me tonight at Luscious? Eight o' clock?"

"I'll be there."

"Thank you." Grace swallows another mouthful of coffee. "Fuckface."

Anytime." I sit back in my seat. "Mouth-breather."

Chapter Thirty-Six

Hayden

"So are you ever going to tell me about her?" Mr. Rose's gruff voice startles me from the filing I'm skimming. I swivel in my chair to face him.

"Hey, Boss." I smirk.

Mr. Rose gives me a kind smile. "Hayden."

"That would be me."

"Who is she?" Mr. Rose asks.

If you're referring to the woman I'm totally falling for, her name is Blake. "Who is who?"

"You've been more...spirited lately. I'm thinking there's a lady involved. Who's the lady?"

I gasp animatedly. "Mr. Rose! That's terribly unprofessional of you to inquire about my personal relations."

Mr. Rose rubs his grayish beard as he chuckles. "That might true, but you're like a daughter to me."

My throat swells with emotion so I swallow it down. Mr. and Mrs. Rose are the closest thing I have to family aside from Ava. Mr. Rose had been friends with my father since they were children and after Evie passed away and my parents left, Mr. Rose and his wife took it upon themselves to make sure I knew I had their support. Mr. Rose gave me a job when I needed one and a place to spend the holidays for the past few years.

"I know you mean that. Thank you," I say.

"I want you to be happy and you seem happy."

"I am happy." I pause, nodding. "I'm also kinda scared though."

Mr. Rose's eyes widen. "Scared, huh? Must be some lady."

I scoff. "You have no idea."

"Fear isn't always our enemy. Often, our enemy is our failure to understand why our response to something is fear. If something is good, you should feel gratitude or joy...not fear. You get to choose how you respond to life. If you respond fearfully, you're going to miss out on a whole lot of living. You dig?"

I laugh. "I understand. I can dig it."

"Good." Mr. Rose gestures behind himself towards the garage. "Back to work, I go." He begins to walk away but then stops and turns to me again. "You know, you should bring her over sometime for dinner. I'll have the wife whip up a batch of those kick-ass brownies."

"Thank you."

Mr. Rose points at me. "Be good."

"Always."

Mr. Rose waves and I watch him disappear into the garage. The bell to the office entrance suddenly sounds forcing my attention to the front door. I spin in my chair to face the door and my heart hurtles over itself multiple times, my breath becomes suspended in my lungs. I can't help but gape.

Blake is standing in the doorway of Rose Family Auto Shop about twenty feet away from me. She has on light blue flared jeans ripped at the knees, a fashionably faded black fitted sweatshirt beneath a pale purple military parka, and brown leather ankle boots. Her wavy, chocolate mane is pulled back into a loose ponytail. Her glossy lips form a kittenish grin as she watches me drink her in. Eventually, my eyes meet hers and she takes off her oversized yet stylish sunglasses. She doesn't greet me though. Instead she gestures to the glass door behind her, where her black sedan is parked.

"I'm sorry to bother you," Blake begins. "But you see, I think there's something wrong with my car, and I was really hoping you could take a look at it."

I run my hand over my mouth to wipe away my smile, stand up from my seat and clear my throat. I step out from behind my desk. "Well, I'm not actually a mechanic," I say. "I just work here."

Blake gives me a once-over and pouts. "That's a crying shame...I for sure thought you were...you know, with hands like yours and all." Blake shakes her head. "Such a waste."

I feel the tips of my ears heat up. "I'm sorry to disappoint you."

Blake steps further into the office and struts towards me. "Don't be sorry. I'm quite confident we could think of another way to put your hands to good use."

I narrow my eyes at her. "Oh yeah? What do you suggest?"

Blake glances around and then her gaze falls back on me.

"Do you get a break?"

"I do."

Blake scrapes her bottom lip with her teeth. "Did you take it yet?"

"No."

"Can you take it now?"

"For you, yes."

Blake smiles. "Is there somewhere we can go?"

I wince. Rose Family Auto is a small business that operates out of an equally small building. "There's a storage room, but it's—"

Blake grabs my hand. "I don't care what it is. Take me there."

"Okay. Let me just tell my boss I'm going on break." I squeeze Blake's hand and as I'm about to let go so that I can yell to Mr. Rose through the garage door, she tightens her grip on me and pulls me into her. She kisses me with such force that I become light-headed. After a moment or perhaps eons, our mouths slowly separate.

"Hi, Hayden," Blake says softly.

I find oxygen. Barely. I smile. "Hi, Blake."

Chapter Thirty-Seven

Blake

I arrive at Luscious with ten minutes to spare before I'm supposed to be meeting up with Grace and her new bae, so I head over to the bar. I text Grace to let her know I'm here and situate myself on a barstool.

"Wouldn't ever think to see you here on a Tuesday," a familiar voice says to the back of my head.

I turn around and smile. "Connor," I greet him. "I could say the same for you."

Connor smirks. "I've been picking up more shifts lately. What's your excuse?"

"Grace wanted me to meet her here tonight. I'm meeting the girlfriend."

"Wow." Connor nods. "Must be serious."

"Considering she's never asked me to meet anyone before, yes. I'm thinking she's serious about this one."

"Beer?"

I purse my lips thoughtfully. "I'm going to be adventurous and go with a vodka tonic."

"Huh."

"What?"

Connor narrows his eyes at me. "You still hanging around Hayden Walcott?"

"Maybe. Why? What's it to you?"

Connor shrugs. "It's just that neither of you tend to...stick around the same woman for very long."

"Well, people change."

"Do they though?" Connor slings his white bar cloth over his shoulder. "I'll be right back with your drink."

Of course people can change. Can't they? Yes. The totally can. I've changed. Haven't I? Ugh. God damnit, Connor.

194

"Blake!" Grace's voice pulls me from my meandering thoughts. I spin around in my seat and my heart momentarily screeches to a standstill. I immediately recognize the blonde hair that belongs to Grace's companion and judging by the way she's gaping at me, she recognizes me also.

I point to Blondie. "Ava?"

Ava beams excitedly. "Blake!"

Grace's eyes dart back and forth between Ava and I until they finally settle on me.

"You two know each other?" Grace asks.

"Sorta," I say.

Grace glares at me. "Tell me you didn't—"

"No!" I hold up both of my hands defensively. "No. Not like that."

"Like how then?" Grace asks.

I hear Connor slide my drink towards me. I reach around for my vodka tonic and take a long sip. I swallow the burn. "We have a mutual friend."

Grace looks at Ava again. "You do?"

Ava's smile somehow gets even wider. "We totally do! Hayden's my best friend and Blake and Hayden… um… hang out sometimes."

Hang out. Ha!

Grace's mouth opens a little and she eyes me once more. "*The* Hayden?"

Christ. Leave it up to Grace to make everything sound scandalous.

I press my lips together and nod. "Mmhm."

"Wow." Grace shakes her head, nonplussed. After a few seconds of uncomfortable silence, Grace clears her throat. "Okay then. Well, in the name of proper formalities…" She puts one of her hands on Ava's shoulder and gestures to me with the other. "Ava, this is my bestie, Blake. And Blake, this is my girlfriend, Ava."

I raise my drink. "Nice to meet you, Ava...again."

Ava purses her smiling lips and nods a small nod. "It's nice to meet you again too, Blake." Then she leans into my personal space and whispers, "I love my new bras." She backs away and winks at me.

Grace apparently overheard her girlfriend because she smirks at me. "The bras," she mouths and gives me a thumbs up.

Can this be over now?

"Ladies," Grace says. "Let's grab ourselves a table." She motions to an empty high-top nearby. Reluctantly, I get off my stool. I reach into my purse, take a few bills from my wallet, and place them on the bar for Connor. I let Grace escort both Ava and I to the table.

I wonder where Hayden is.

Once we're all seated, Grace points in the general direction of the bathrooms. She places her hand on top of Ava's. "I have to hit the restroom," Grace informs Ava. "Think about what you might want to drink."

Grace looks at me. "I'll be back."

The fuck? You better be back.

"Okay," I say and watch Grace fade into the large crowd standing between us and the bathrooms.

"This is crazy that you're Grace's best friend," Ava says.

I turn to face Ava and force a smile. "So crazy."

"Don't tell Hayden that I told you this but she really likes you."

Yeah but she loves you so you win. "Did she say that?"

"I can just tell."

"Right."

"Blake." Ava stares at me intently.

"Yes?"

"Hayden's a good person. Don't hurt her."

Whoa. Protective much? "I know she's a good person." *Which is why I'd ask her out if she weren't so fucking hung up on your blonde ass.*

Ava places her hand on my arm and leans closer to me. "I'm not trying to be a bitch. She's my family. I care about her."

"I care about her too." I shrug. "More than I ever really wanted to."

Ava smiles at me. "Yeah. She has that effect on people."

I return the smile. "It's annoying as fuck."

Ava and I share a chuckle. "It's totally annoying."

I drink more of my vodka tonic. "In a slightly charming way...but I never said that."

"You never said what?" Ava winks at me.

It's very easy for me to see why Hayden has a thing for Ava...she's extremely likeable. A sick sadness roils my belly. I know now that I don't stand a chance with Hayden.

"Alright, girls!" Grace shouts a little too loudly as she approaches our table. "What are we drinking?"

I'm sitting next to the woman who Hayden is in love with and I'm full of envy because I'm not her. *All the drinks. I want all the drinks.*

Chapter Thirty-Eight

Hayden

I finally decide on a movie from the DVD collection neatly piled on the shelf below the living room television. I struggle to get the case open and as soon as I succeed, my phone vibrates. I know it's not Blake because she mentioned something about having plans tonight and I know it's not Ava because she has a date tonight. Although maybe Blake wrapped up her plans early and she's now texting me for some quality sexy time. I grin to myself and pluck my phone from my pocket. I furrow my brow when I see that the text is from Connor.

Hey. I'm working and you may or may not want to come down here.

I squint at my phone's screen; at Connor's words and then respond.

Why?

Connor's reply pops up instantly.

I don't mean to be a drag, but I thought you should see this.

I stare at Connor's text and then at the blank box where what I think is going to be a picture that's attempting to load as an attachment will appear. I wait. I'm not sure why but I feel queasy. Connor rarely texts me. *Why the hell is this picture taking so freaking long to upload?!* I begin cussing at my phone and suddenly the blank box is gone. It's been replaced by a picture. I stare at the photo and shake my head. *No. This isn't possible.* I blink deliberately and look at the picture again. My gut twists violently. My breath stays lodged in my tightened chest. *How is this possible?*

Slowly, tears that I refuse to set free blur the image on my phone, but it makes no difference. The image is already seared into my mind: Ava and Blake sitting inordinately close together. Ava's leaning into Blake; her hand is on Blake's arm. Blake is smiling. I close my eyes and wish the picture away. I open my eyes and it's still there, staring back at me. Mocking me. I cover my hand over my mouth and nearly sprint to the bathroom. I drop to my knees in front of the toilet and vomit. Once I'm done throwing up, I have every intention of getting up and going to Luscious to confront Ava and Blake. Except I don't. When I'm done emptying the contents of my stomach, I hold onto to the edges of the toilet seat and begin to cry.

I arrive at Luscious about forty minutes after receiving Connor's text. I was sure to clean myself up and rehearse my tirade several times before exiting Leela, my station wagon. But when I walk through the entrance of the bar, I forget everything I was going to say to Blake and Ava. *Son of a bitch.* I take a breath and steel myself before I start making my way through the bar. I really want to go home and sob until sleep overcomes me. Instead, I roll my shoulders back and hold my head up high.

I take a step forward. A group of drunken girls bump into me and grab onto each other to hold themselves up. They giggle out an apology. I sneer at them, brush my clammy palms along the front of my green utility jacket, and keep moving. It takes me less than a minute to spot them and it only takes that same amount of time for my heart to sink. Blake, Ava and some woman with long, aubergine red hair who I've never seen before are sitting at a high-top table in one of the more secluded sections of the bar. The red haired woman finishes saying something and Blake and Ava laugh. My insides sour. I pause a few feet from the table before I go up to them.

My mouth is ridiculously dry, but I manage to force down a swallow. Then I stride over to their table. Blake sees me before anyone else. She does a double take and when it registers that it's me she's looking at, her eyes light up in a way that throws me off. *Concentrate.* I inhale deeply and glare at her. She stares at me quizzically. I place my hand on the table, making my presence known.

"Hey," Blake says to me. I ignore her.

"Hayden!" Ava squeals and grabs my arm, but I pull away.

"So, this is Hayden," The red haired woman says, smiling.

Now, both Blake and Ava are looking at me with worried expressions. The red haired woman must feel the eeriness around her because her smile quickly evaporates.

"Yes. I'm Hayden," I say to the woman with red hair.

"I thought you were staying in tonight," Ava says.

"What's going on?"

"Why don't you tell me?"

Ava flinches. "What?"

I retrieve my phone from the back pocket of my jeans and swipe the screen. When the picture of Blake and Ava appears, I rest my phone on the table.

"Don't play me," I snap at Ava. "What is this?" I finally turn to Blake, who's studying the photo on my phone. "Is there something you guys want to tell me?"

Blake looks at me, shaking her head. "What the fuck is this? Where did you get this?"

"You tell me what the fuck this is!" I reclaim my phone. "You're on a date with my best friend. Behind my back. Why?"

Blake opens her mouth to speak, but Ava beats her to it.

"Whoa!" Ava waves her arms in the air. "No. Hayden, it's not—"

I immediately redirect my attention from Blake to Ava and point my finger in Ava's face, scowling at her. "You." My voice is low. "You know I have feelings for her…" I motion to Blake without looking away from Ava. "You even set me up that day at the mall so that I could see her and yet here you are. On a date with her."

"Dude!" Ava smacks my hand from her face. "I am not here on a date with Blake."

I hold my phone up. "Don't lie to me. I have photographic evidence."

"No. What you have is a picture that proves absolutely nothing," Ava says. "Calm down so we can sort this out."

"What kinds of feelings do you have for me?" Blake asks.

I step back from the table. I feel myself unraveling. I have to leave. I cannot cry with an audience.

Blake gets out of her seat and reaches for me, but I move further away. "Hayden? Will you please answer my question?"

"It doesn't matter anymore," I say softly.

"Hayden, stay. We'll figure this out," Ava says.

I scoff and shake my head despondently. "There's nothing to figure out. This picture Connor sent me says it all. At least someone gives a fuck about me." My eyes bounce between Ava and Blake one last time and I nod. I turn my back to them and start walking hurriedly towards the exit. From somewhere behind me, I hear Blake call out my name right when I get to the door. Her voice rattles my bones and my legs nearly give out. I want to stop for her, but I don't. I grit my teeth as fresh tears begin to sting my cheeks. I make it outside and break into a run.

Chapter Thirty-Nine

Blake

"Hayden!" I yell again after her once I'm outside of Luscious, but she keeps running.

I toss my head back. "Aargh!" *Fuck my life.* Ava materializes at my side, panting.

"Grace is paying the tab," Ava says. "I'm going to have her take me home. I'll wait for Hayden there, but you should be the one to go after her."

I draw my eyebrows together in confusion. "I don't understand. Why don't I just go to your place with you and Grace? We could talk to her once she gets home."

Ava shakes her head. "She's not going to go home. Not right away, but I'll be sure to be there when she does."

"If she's not going home then where is she going?"

"I'll text you the address."

Panic suddenly surges through me. "Wait. Shouldn't you be the one to go after her? She loves you."

"If you don't have any feelings for her at all then yes, I'll go."

What the...? Is this a trap? Is this broad trapping me? I sigh. "Well yeah I have feelings...but she loves *you.*"

Ava gives me a small smile and places her hand on my shoulder. She squeezes. "Trust me. You should be the one to go after her."

"Fine. Text me that address and I'll go, but there's something I have to do first."

I lean over the far right side of the bar.

"Hey, Connor!" I holler. When Connor looks at me, I flash him a winsome smile and use my index finger to signal for him to come to me. He smirks at me and promptly starts towards me.

When Connor gets to where I'm standing, he leans in close to me. "Ms. Caruso, what can I do for you?" He asks.

I press my lips together and raise my eyebrows. "You could be honest with me."

Connor's forehead creases. "Huh?"

"Did you or did you not send Hayden a picture of me with her friend, Ava?"

"I did."

"Mmhm. And why would you do that?"

"Blake, I care about you."

"Do you want an award?"

Connor frowns. "What? No."

"Then answer my fucking question."

Connor rolls his eyes. "I sent her the picture to protect you."

I gasp. "To protect me?"

"Yes."

"To protect me from what?"

"Hayden," Connor says. "She doesn't know how to keep it in her pants. Eventually, she would've hurt you and you deserve better."

"Do I?"

The lines in Connor's brow deepen. "Um. Yeah."

"Since when did you get to decide what I deserve?"

"Blake, I'm only saying that she's a player. She uses women."

"Dude, apparently you lost the memo. I'm a player too. And although I can't speak for all players, I can tell you with certainty that Hayden and I don't 'use' women...we appreciate them...on a sexual level." I shake my head. "Also, you were the one who encouraged me to talk to her. Why would you do that if you thought I needed protection from her?"

"I thought maybe you two would hook up. Then you'd come back and thank me, and you and I could talk more."

I hold my hand up. "Whoa. Hold up. And what exactly would I be thanking you for?"

Connor shrugs. "I heard she's a good lay."

Instinctively, I slap him across the face. The sound of my palm against Connor's cheek causes several patrons to silence themselves and stare in our direction.

"Ow! Fuck!" Connor smooths his hand across his face and flexes his jaw.

"You're a bitch, you know that?" I seethe.

"Blake, I'm sorry. I just wanted to talk to you more."

"And that was the best plan you could come up with?"

"Yes."

"What is your damage, dude?"

"Nothing. I like you."

I gape. "You what now?"

"I like you," Connor repeats. "I never stopped liking you."

"Let me see if I'm understanding this. So you thought that if I had amazing sex with someone, Hayden to be more specific, courtesy of you then you'd be a hero to me or something? And then I'd come here and tell you how much I appreciate you and then...what? We'd chum it up and I'd magically become straight and have a hard on for you?"

Connor purses his lips ponderously. "Kind of."

I nod. "You know it was your dick that made me realize I was a flaming dyke, right?"

Connor pales.

"But your genius plan failed because why would it not? And then you needed to figure out another way to...keep me unattached?"

Connor looks right at me as his eyebrows jerk upwards. He gives me an arrogant half-smile.

"Psycho!" I exclaim and slap him again.

"Damnit, Blake!"

We've drawn a crowd now. A large man in a suit appears from the back of the bar.

"Tamblyn!" The large man shouts at Connor. "If you continue to cause a scene in my establishment, you're going to be unemployed."

Connor turns to the man I'm assuming is his boss. "Sorry, Sir." Connor then faces me. "You have to go," he says under his breath.

"No."

"Blake," Connor hisses.

"Way back when, were you the one who posted that picture all over social media of Sarah and A.J. kissing?"

Connor closes his eyes for a long second and then meets my gaze. "Yes."

I swallow back the sickness making its way up my throat. "How did you get ahold of the picture?"

Connor shakes his head. "I took it."

Without hesitation, I sucker punch Connor in the nose. "You motherfucker!"

Connor yelps in pain and quickly places the bar cloth over his nose. There's uproar among the herd of people surrounding us.

"Tamblyn! Enough! You're out!" The large man bellows at Connor.

"If you really care about me, you'll make this right." I lower my head and shake it. "And get a therapist while you're at it," I mumble to him. I pretend not to feel the dull throb shooting up my right arm and flounce out of the bar.

As soon as I sit behind the wheel of my car, I pull my phone from my pocket. I read the text that Ava sent me and program the address into my GPS. I then attempt to call Hayden for the fifth time since she hightailed it out of Luscious earlier. My call goes straight to voicemail. *Ugh!*

"Hayden, hi. It's me, Blake...again. Please talk to me." I hang up the phone and start the engine. "Hayden, please," I whisper.

Chapter Forty

Hayden

I hold my phone close to my ear and listen to Blake's fifth voice message. Once it's over, I replay it. Then I go to replay it again, but an incoming text message interrupts me. The text is from Connor. I exhale heavily and open the message.

I sent you that picture to fuck with you. I was jealous of you. I like Blake. It was a dick move and she definitely let me know that. I'm sorry.

"What?" I gasp. *No. No. No. I did not just make a complete ass of myself for no reason. This cannot be my life.* Instantaneously, I recount my confrontation with Blake and Ava at Luscious; all the false accusations I made. I cringe. *Shit.* I glare at the screen of my phone and reread Connor's message. I'm shaking with anger. I try to compose a response with unsteady fingers, but before I even finish spelling the first word, there's a knock at the front door. My eyes glance to the cable box clock on top of the television in the Rose's living room. It's a little past eleven o' clock. I'm pretty sure Mr. and Mrs. Rose aren't expecting any visitors considering they both went to bed over an hour ago. There's another knock. This one is more demanding. *Should I answer the door to someone else's house? Is that appropriate? What if it's a burglar? Would a burglar knock? Probably not...*

Mr. Rose suddenly appears in the living room. He's in his bathrobe and holding a baseball bat. His eyes are fixed on the front door. He looks to me.

"Did you invite someone here?" Mr. Rose whispers.

"No."

He points to me, sprawled out across his loveseat. "You stay there." He raises the bat over his left shoulder as if he's ready to hit a line drive and steps closer to the door. Mrs. Rose emerges from the kitchen holding up a stainless steel frying pan with one hand, a cordless phone in the other. Feeling as though I, too, should be prepared to attack an intruder, I sit up on the sofa. Another knock.

"Hayden!" Blake's voice resounds from the other side of the door, quickening my pulse. "If you're in there, please open up."

Mr. Rose looks at me curiously. I rise from my seat. "It's fine."

Mrs. Rose lowers her pan and Mr. Rose sets his baseball bat against the wall by the entrance. He pulls his bathrobe tighter around himself, reaches for the door handle and opens the door a crack.

"May I help you?" Mr. Rose asks Blake.

"Hi." I can hear Blake from where I'm standing but I can't see her because Mr. Rose is obstructing my view. "Are you Mr. Rose?"

"I am."

"I'm so sorry to bother you this late but I'm looking for someone. Hayden Walcott. I was told by her friend, Ava, that she might be here. Is she?"

"And you are?" Mr. Rose asks even though he and Mrs. Rose already know who Blake is because I might have mentioned her in passing. Like a thousand times.

"My name is Blake."

Mr. Rose nods and opens the door all the way. "Come on inside." He motions towards the living room. To me. Blake steps cautiously into Mr. and Mrs. Rose's home. She offers Mr. Rose a small, grateful smile and then turns to me.

"Why are you here?" I ask her.

"Hayden, please hear me out. There's been a huge misunderstanding. I can explain everything if you'll let me."

I hold up my phone. "I already know. Connor just texted me his confession."

"So he told you that..." Blake glimpse shyly at Mr. and Mrs. Rose and then her big, brown eyes fall back on me. "He told you that Ava and I were not on a date?"

"Not in so many words, but yeah."

Blake lets out a breath and runs her right hand through her hair.

I notice the discoloration on Blake's knuckles. *She's hurt. How?*

"I'm sorry for blowing up on you the way I did. Really, I am."

"It's okay. I get it," Blake chews on her bottom lip for a second and then continues. "Hayden, I would never do that to you," she says. "I know how you feel about Ava."

Mr. Rose clears his throat and I can see the pointed look he's giving me in my peripheral vision. *I knew I confided in him way too much.*

"About that," I begin. "There's something I have to tell you."

Concern clouds Blake's expression. "What?"

I look at Mr. And Mrs. Rose. "I appreciate your hospitality, but I should go."

"Anytime, Hayden," Mr. Rose says.

I walk over to Mr. and Mrs. Rose, who are now standing side by side, and give them each a hug. Then I face Blake.

"What's going on?" Blake asks.

"Will you go somewhere with me? Somewhere more...private?"

"Where?"

I shrug. "Anywhere. I'm open to ideas."

Blake nods. "Do you want to come home with me?"

The flutter in my heart is so intense it gives me chills.

"Yes."

Chapter Forty-One

Blake

I step inside my dungeon-dark living quarters and flick the lights on. I purposely leave the door unlocked for Hayden, who I gather will be arriving at any time now. The visitor's lot of the condominium complex was uncommonly crowded so it might take her an extra few minutes to find a spot. I have no idea what she wants to talk to me about, but I'm trying to stay cool; keep my wits about me and all that jazz. I tell myself not to pace, but I do anyways. Pacing isn't helpful though. It only reminds me that my kitchen floor is overdue for a mopping. A soft rap at my door draws my eyes away from the floor.

"Blake?" Hayden's voice echoes from within the hallway.

"It's open," I respond and needlessly begin rifling through the stack of neglected mail on the kitchen island to make it look as if I were doing something other than simply waiting for Hayden's arrival even though that's exactly what I was doing. I feel Hayden's presence enter my space. I hear the click of the door closing behind her. I put down the pile of sealed envelopes and acknowledge Hayden with a strained smile.

Hayden smiles back. "Thanks for this...for asking me to come over."

"Sure. So what is it that you wanted to tell me?"

Hayden walks towards me. "I've been thinking a lot about our...friendship, and I..." Hayden swallows. "I can't do it anymore."

My chest locks up. My heart plummets into my stomach. *I should have seen that coming. Shit. I am such an idiot for even tampering with the idea that maybe Hayden liked me as much as I like her. Ugh. Alright. Don't cry.*

211

"Okay." *Unemotional response. That was good.*

"I'm not done," Hayden says.

Christ almighty. "Listening."

"Blake, I can't be your friend anymore because when I'm with you, I feel like...I feel everything. I feel so many things that I've never felt before, not even with Ava, and it's scary and uncomfortable but it's amazing and I can appreciate if you don't feel the same. I can. I mean, we agreed on a friend with benefits thing, but it's too hard for me. I don't want to be your fuck friend. I want to be your girlfriend."

I breathe in sharply. *Seriously? You couldn't have lead with that? You just had to open with something cryptic, didn't you? Fucking A, woman. And also, do you really not know?* Hayden's staring at me apprehensively with her crystal blue eyes. *Nope. She really doesn't know. Alright then. I guess it's my turn.* My heart is beating so hard against my chest that I'm sure she can hear it. "How long have you felt this way?"

Hayden shrugs shyly. The tips of her ears are flaming red. "I don't know exactly. I only know that ever since I met you, I couldn't ever seem to get enough of you. Then I got confused because I thought I was in love with Ava, but I...what I feel for you is so different. And you said that if a person has to ask themselves if they're in love or not, they're probably not. Because of you...how you make me feel, I've been asking myself that about Ava. And I'm sure now that Ava was right, I was never in love with her. Infatuated, yes. But you...you got to me, and I'm tired of pretending that you don't. I'm tired of fighting it."

"Is this the reason you asked me for my thoughts on love? Because you weren't certain about your feelings for Ava?"

"Yeah."

"And Ava thinks you aren't in love with her?"

"Yeah. She thinks that I'm...um...she knows me real well is all."

I nod, silently wondering what she's not telling me. Although it was Ava who practically insisted that *I* be the one to chase after Hayden earlier this evening. *Hmm.*

"When you showed me the picture that Connor sent you, I was ready to break his neck...because I saw the hurt in your eyes," I begin. "And it didn't matter whether you were hurt because of me or because of Ava or because of both of us. It only mattered to me that you were hurt and I was part of the reason and knowing that was the worst feeling."

Hayden's forehead creases into a V shape. "That's all cleared up now."

"Right, but see...a lifetime ago, I gave my heart away." *You can do this. Tell her.*

"To Sarah?"

Ugh. That name. "Yes. To Sarah. And one day, I was killing time online or whatever and I spot this picture on Cyberjournal...of Sarah making out with some girl...some girl that definitely wasn't me. But my name was the caption above that photographic gem. That picture was posted specifically for me to see...but that wasn't the worst part. The worst part was that all my friends saw it too. That picture was everywhere on social media in under ten minutes and just like that I became known as a chump. I was the girl who could be fooled and fucked over." I press my lips together. "So I confronted her. She swore up and down that the picture had been photoshopped. She went on some spiel about how she'd never cheat on me. This was amusing to me because the thing is, I had already confronted A.J, the girl she was kissing in the picture, before I confronted her. And A.J. confessed. I listen to Sarah babble on and then I told her that I had talked to A.J. Sarah started crying. Apologizing. And I just walked away. I had Grace get my belongings from Sarah's place and I took all of Sarah's belongings that I had and put them in the dumpster. Sarah and I never spoke again. And I spent a lot of time and energy building walls around my heart since then. I got walls for days, Hayden. There it is: I'm admittedly emotionally stunted." *There's my sob story; my damage. Take me or leave me.* I glance at my unmopped floor for a moment to myself. *Please take me.* I look back up at Hayden.

The corners of Hayden's mouth turn down. "I'm sorry that that was your experience, but someone wise once told me that everyone's a little fucked up."

"She must be a god damned genius."

Hayden chuckles briefly. "Obviously." Her expression sobers. "Hey, I told you that I wouldn't hurt you."

"Those are just words. The reality of life is that people will hurt you. If you're going to actually make the decision to take a chance and live this life, you have to accept that there is a possibility of pain that comes with that."

"People will hurt you, yes, but not everyone."

"No. Maybe not everyone."

"Maybe I won't." Hayden steps closer to me.

"Maybe you will."

"If you let me, maybe I can break down your walls."

There it is. I scrape my bottom lip with my top teeth and smirk. "You wanna break down my walls, do you?"

Hayden smiles a little. "I do…if you want me to."

"And how would you go about doing that?"

"Well first I'd ask you to be my girlfriend."

"Ah. Is that so?"

"It is."

I fold my arms across my chest. "I'm waiting."

Hayden reaches out and eases my arms away from my chest. She holds my hands in hers.

"Blake, will you be my girlfriend?"

I grab the neck of Hayden's flannel shirt and pull her to me. "You dork, you already broke down my walls so yeah, you can bet your fine ass I'll be your girlfriend." I kiss Hayden's grinning lips, completely sealing the distance between us.

Chapter Forty-Two

Hayden

As soon as Blake's soft lips are against mine, I stop grinning. I shut my eyes and open my mouth a little to intensify the kiss. Blake reciprocates and our tongues stroke one another's in a slow, circular motion. I cup her face in my hands and her fingers begin to wrestle with the buttons of my shirt.

"Bed," Blake pants and gives me a gentle push backwards, steering me towards her room. We resume kissing. Our mouths are equally warm and eager. Blake finishes unfastening my shirt. Her hands instantly find my skin. She slips her arms around my waist and we continue fumbling backwards to get to her bedroom. We stumble over a footrest in the living room and laugh, our lips vibrating against each other's for a second until we regain our balance. We hold onto one another to steady ourselves and our mouths rediscover their rhythm. We start staggering again, dodging most of the furniture in our path until we finally step through the threshold of Blake's bedroom.

It only takes a few steps before the backs of my calves are pressed into the box spring of Blake's mattress. She slides my shirt off of my shoulders and it falls to the floor. She reaches behind me and unhooks my bra. She eases the straps down my arms and does away with it. At a tauntingly slow pace, Blake's flattened palms explore my exposed chest. She's sure to run her thumbs over my nipples, which causes us both to gasp. Eventually, her fingers make their way to my pants. She ignores the button and zipper altogether and takes full advantage of the fact that they've got a little stretch to them. She hitches them down, past my hips and then lets them go. They pool around my ankles. She draws her index fingers back up my outer thighs. Her touch gives me chills. When I shiver, I can feel her smirk against my lips. I comb my hands through Blake's long, brown tresses, rest them on the back of her neck and pull her closer to me. Her trimmed fingernails trace the rim of my boy shorts and the ache between my legs becomes unforgiving.

I grab the hem of Blake's sweatshirt. With much disinclination, I tear my lips from Blake's. "Arms up," I say quietly.

Blake lifts her arms straight up as if she's trying to touch the ceiling. I inch her top up over her head, her arms. She yanks the sleeves off of her wrists and throws the shirt to the side. I wrestle the fastener of her black, scoop demi bra. Once it's unclasped, Blake slips her bra off and discards it. Our mouths meet again. Our breaths are heavy between ravenous kisses.

I gently touch Blake's chest before I begin kneading her breasts. She gasps into my mouth and nips my bottom lip with her teeth. I unsnap her jeans and start to wriggle them over her waist. Blake breaks our kiss and impulsively kicks off her boots and removes her bottoms. I steal a glimpse of her rose colored fishnet thong. *I can't even with the hotness.* Blake catches me ogling her when she's finished stripping. She supplies me with a fiendish grin.

"I'll let you take those off," she says, her voice husky. I lay my hands on her hips, ready to oblige, but she places her hand on my bare chest and nudges me backwards, onto the bed. She follows me. Once my backside is pressed into the mattress, Blake positions herself on top of me; her knees denting the comforter on either side of my body. She reaches behind herself and blindly does away with my sneakers. Then she pulls at the ankles of my pants until they're completely off.

Each of us is left with only our underwear on.

Blake stares down at me. Her eyes darken as they peruse the length of my body. She draws a circle around my belly button with her finger, her gaze trained on my face. When I flinch, she smiles at me. She lowers her head and suddenly I feel her lips on my stomach. Then she runs her tongue up my abdomen, along the swell of my breasts, my collarbone, my neck. I close my eyes the moment her mouth is on mine. I part my lips to indulge the kiss. Blake's weight on top of me feels like the most natural thing; our skin fusing together. A small whimper escapes me when Blake's body begins to writhe against mine. Our kiss is primal now. I can hardly catch my breath. My head presses even further into the mattress when Blake eases herself just the slightest bit off me; her body shifting to my left side. I instantly miss the heat of her flesh, but only for a second because as soon as Blake's right forefingers begin to trail the insides of my thighs, I become delirious.

Blake slows our kiss and I match her pace. I savor the softness of her lips, the way her tongue caresses mine. I listen to our labored breaths, my heartbeat thrumming between my ears. The pleasure within me builds even more. Blake hooks her fingers in the waistband of my boy briefs and with painstaking care, she edges them down my legs. Then there's a momentary break in our kiss. Blake's gaze drifts across my face until we lock eyes. She bites her bottom lip and half-smiles, shaking her head.

"I'm so yours," Blake whispers.

My heart nearly implodes inside my chest. So many feels. I return the smile. "Same."

Blake nods deliberately as she lowers her face to mine. Her mouth covers my mouth again. My eyes flutter shut. She smooths her hand along my side, to the junction of my thighs. I instinctively spread my legs and when Blake's fingers graze my warm, wet sex, everything gets a little hazy.

Blake gasps and I release a low moan. She carefully enters me and my hips buckle. She finds my G-spot in seconds and pulses her fingers against it.

"Fuck," I groan into our kiss. I lift my pelvis off the mattress and push myself against her touch to increase the pressure. Her fingers beat inside me in flawless measures for a long minute then she slides her digits from me and runs them back over my clit. Every muscle in my body tightens. Blake eases her lips away from mine and I open my eyes. She arrests me with her stare as her lithe fingers massage the place I ache the most. My stomach catapults.

Blake's forehead is shiny with perspiration. Her lips are more red than pink. Her pupils are dilated, nearly swallowing the beautiful light brown tones in her irises. She's so beautiful, it almost hurts to look at her. There's a glint of desire in her eyes as her fingers throb against me methodically. All of me tenses. I close my eyes and my throat unleashes a shallow groan as an orgasm washes over me with such force, I reach up and hold onto Blake, my fingernails digging into her shoulder blades.

When my body relaxes, my arms drop and I grab onto Blake's wrist to keep it still. I'm far too sensitive to withstand her touch right now. I catch my breath and swallow. I open my eyes. Blake is watching me, smiling. Her gorgeousness...it is almost other worldly. I am mesmerized. I gasp a laugh and shake my head while a few stray tears cascade down the sides of my face.

"You," I manage.

Blake wipes away my tears with her thumb and plants a gentle kiss on the corner of my mouth.

"No. You."

Chapter Forty-Three

Blake

Hayden grabs me by the waist and playfully wrestles me onto my back. I wrap my arms around her neck so that when I collapse on the mattress, I pull her down with me. Her chest is flush against mine. Our bodies are sticky with sweat. It's beyond sexy.

"Trying to top me?" I smirk.

"Yes." Hayden buries her nose in the dip between the right side of my neck and collarbone. Her lips prickle my skin with a small kiss. Then she aligns her face with mine. "Are you okay with that?"

I lick my lips. "I'm very okay with that."

Hayden smiles and pecks the tip of my nose, careful of the stud in my nostril. The gesture is so innocent, so tender, that it makes my heart swell. I place my hands on her cheeks and kiss her on her perfect mouth. It's only when she parts her lips and gingerly slips her tongue inside my mouth that there's a whoosh in my belly and my pulse accelerates. I exhale a surprised sigh into Hayden's mouth. I rake my fingers through the layers of her hair and bite down on her thick bottom lip. *That lip.* Passion quickly begins to orchestrate the tempo of our kiss. In seconds, we're breathless and groping each other frantically.

Hayden slides her hands to my hips and by degrees, our kiss slowly comes to a stop. Her lips then begin to tour my jawline, my shoulders, my chest. I shut my eyes. She tenderly fondles my breasts and I silently plead for more of her touch. Her mouth soon replaces her hand and she flicks her tongue against my nipples. *Good god.* I involuntarily squirm with delight beneath her. Then her kisses land on my stomach. She licks a line across it. When her mouth reaches my waist, I feel the heat of her breath. An unexpected thrill rocks through me when she sinks her canines into my flesh and sucks just long enough to leave a magnificent mark. I tilt my head back and unintentionally groan. After Hayden leaves her impression, her lips continue to wander further down my body.

I part my legs, an invitation. Without hesitancy, Hayden positions herself on her knees, my legs on either side of her. She kisses me between my thighs, over the fabric of my thongs. I feel her breath quicken, a likely reaction to how wet I am. Her excitement only serves to amplify my own. In one graceful motion, she slips my panties off and drops them by my feet. Her eyes are the brightest blue as she takes in my naked form. She runs her hands over my legs and grabs my calves. She places a single kiss on the inside of my right thigh, then the left. She passes her tongue along my center. I moan and reach down. I feel Hayden's sweat-dampened hair. I grab a tuft and pull. I open my eyes to watch her taste me. As if she can feel my fixed stare on her, Hayden raises her gaze to mine. Neither of us look away as her tongue swirls around my clit. My heart is palpitating ferociously. I might die. The hotness factor is practically unbearable. Hayden braids her fingers through mine so that we're holding hands.

Suddenly, she picks up momentum, increasing the friction. I gasp and blink for a lengthy second until I'm sure I'll be able to see straight again. Hayden's eyes are still on me, ready to reconnect with mine. I clench my jaw as Hayden's tongue slides up and down my center but before I can catch my breath, she begins soothing her tongue over my arousal but with even more fervor than before. *I'm definitively going to die.* The tension in my body is incredible. I squeeze my pelvic muscles together and start to move my body in time with Hayden's working mouth. I can feel the pulsing between my legs. My head is spinning. My body begins to shake against Hayden's tongue. I close my eyes. I have to as a hot, tingly sensation gushes through me and I erupt. I come hard into Hayden's mouth, my guttural moan echoing within the bedroom walls. My ears are ringing. *Holy shit.* My breathing is heavy as fuck but as it slowly becomes regular, I open my eyes to look at Hayden. She's grinning something amazing while she wipes her hand over her mouth to dry it a little. She moves forward, hovering over me. When our bodies are parallel, Hayden lowers her lips to my lips and we kiss. Once the kiss comes to an end, I smile at her.

"You," I murmur, mimicking Hayden from earlier.

Hayden releases a soft chuckle. "No. You."

"I hope you know that I'm not done with you yet."

"Oh. No?"

"Nope."

"When will you be done with me?"

Never. "When you do you think you'll want me to be done with you?"

"I'm thinking I don't want you be done with me."

I laugh. "I'm thinking we can probably work something out." The tips of Hayden's ears turn red. This will forever be adorable to me. She takes my hands in hers and brushes her left thumb over my right knuckles.

"How'd you get this bruise?" Hayden asks. "I noticed it before but didn't say anything. I was distracted."

I gape theatrically. "You saw that I was injured but you were too 'distracted' to mention it? What in heaven's name could be so important that it distracts you from my wound?"

Hayden snickers. "Your angelic beauty. Obvi."

I laugh again. "You're a goof."

"No. Really though. What happened?"

"Connor and I had words and I defended my lady's honor is what happened." A deep blush colors Hayden's cheeks and she smiles shyly. *D'aww.*

"So I'm your lady, am I?" She asks.

"Aren't you?"

Hayden smirks. "Yeah I am."

I nod and touch my left palm to her face. "Yes. You are."

Chapter Forty-Four

Hayden

I wring my sweaty palms together as I look out at the sea of adolescent faces staring silently at me standing in the front of the classroom. I had paused to gather myself after sharing my story. Ava's sitting in the front row of desks, giving me a thumbs up and an encouraging smile.

I clear my throat and continue. "So, if you or anyone you know might be in trouble, please ask for help or visit the website that I've written on the blackboard." I glance to the back of the room, where Blake and Grace are seated. Blake nods at me. I nod back and focus on my audience of teenagers once again. "Substance addiction is nothing to be ashamed of, but it's a serious epidemic and people lose their lives because of it. I lost my sister because of it. I don't want any of you to lose your lives or to lose anyone you care about because of it. There are people who want to help you so let them." I inhale. "Thank you."

Ava practically jumps out of her seat and takes a stand next to me at the front of the classroom. "Okay, class, I think our guest speaker deserves a round of applause!" Ava begins clapping and slowly the sound of hands against hands fills the room even though there are also some obvious angsty teen eyerolls.

Blake and Grace take it upon themselves to inappropriately whistle while they applaud. I feel the burn of my blush as I glare at them but all I can see is Blake smiling back at me. My unease immediately fades.

I give the kids a tight-lipped smile and curt nod before I take my seat beside the podium for the question and answer portion of this gig. I take a breath. *Happy Birthday, Evie.*

"Cheers!" I raise my shot glass of whiskey. "To Evie." Ava, Grace and Blake all lift their glasses and we clink them together.

"To Evie," Blake repeats.

"And to the best guest speaker Samson Prep has ever had!" Ava hollers.

"A true rockstar." Blake winks at me.

"Word!" Grace whoops and then downs her drink. The rest of us follow her lead and polish off our celebratory shots post-haste.

Ava coughs after she swallows. "Sooo Grace and I have something to tell you guys."

Blake and I exchange puzzled looks then turn our attention to Ava and Grace, who are seated across from us at Blake's dining room table.

"We're moving in together," Grace blurts wearing a huge grin. I gasp and stare slack-jawed at Ava.

Blake points to Grace and lets out a loud, "Ha!"

"For real?" I ask Ava.

Grace puts her arm over Ava's shoulder. "I asked her to move in with me."

Ava beams. "And I said, 'yes'!"

She seems so happy that I have to smile. "Wow. That's huge."

"Seriously." Blake chuckles. "You're totally U-hauling!"

Ava gapes. "What?! It's been three months."

I laugh. "Yeah. U-hauling."

"Well we love each other so…" Grace holds up both of her middle fingers at me and Blake.

Blake snickers and returns the gesture, but only to Grace. "Floosy," she says.

"Shitlicker," Grace retorts.

Ava and I share an amused chuckle.

"Well, I'm happy for you," I say to Ava and Grace.

"As am I," Blake says. She then promptly refills all of our shot glasses and raises hers. "Cheers!"

I look to my left at Blake. My chest swells. *This woman.* The rest of us lift our glasses and in unison, exclaim another, "Cheers!"

Once we're all finished with our drinks, I lean over and whisper into Blake's ear. "Are we still on for our date this week?"

Blake smirks at me. "Wouldn't miss it for the world." I smile at the thought of our upcoming date and then I silently wish for a million more after it.

Chapter Forty-Five

Blake

"Compliments of the blonde woman to your right," The new bartender at Luscious says as she places a glass of the house porter on a coaster in front of me.

I give the bartender a genial smile. "Thank you." She tips her head at me as if to say 'you're welcome' and then ambles over to the other side of the bar to assist other patrons.

It's almost nine o'clock on a Friday night so the crowds are starting to file in now. On the rare occasion that I find myself in a bar or a club, I enjoy people-watching, but I'm not here for them on this particular evening. I'm here for her. I slowly turn my gaze to the right and at the woman casually approaching me, a vodka tonic in her grasp. I appraise her from head to toe and fight to keep my jaw muscles taut to curb an oncoming smile. Instead, I just leer.

She's wearing a black button down shirt with light gray suspenders fastened to a pair of men's skinny jeans. Her classic all-white basketball sneakers are spotless. Her sophisticated bob is perfectly producted, but not overly so, which allows me to make out the multi-dimensional tones blended throughout her sandy colored hair. The longer layers of her locks fall against her jawline in a way that compliments her oval-shaped face. *Definitely a hottie.* Butterflies swarm through my stomach. I catch my breath, thinking about what it feels like to run my fingers through her hair, knowing what the tattoos look like beneath her black button down.

Hayden's finally standing in front of me. Her crystal blue eyes are gleaming. I allow myself to be devoured by their bright lightness. *Sigh.*

She smiles at me, a fitted hoop ring decorating the left side of her thick, lower lip. *That lip.* I desperately want to bite it. And I will. Later.

Hayden raises her glass of vodka tonic and makes a gesture towards my beer.

"Aren't you gonna drink that?" She asks.

I quirk a skeptical eyebrow at Hayden. "Ohh. You're the one who sent this over, yes?"

"Yes. That would be me. I mean porter *is* your drink, is it not?"

"It is." I swivel in my barstool to fully face Hayden. "I'm sorry. Do I know you?"

Hayden slides onto the stool next to mine. "No, but you will."

I snort. "Will I?"

"Yes. You will."

"Are you hitting on me?"

"I am." Hayden flashes me a grin. "How am I doing?"

I nod slowly, my lips pursed. "Pretty fucking good actually."

"Good." Hayden motions again to my beer. "It's going to get warm."

I offer Hayden a small smirk and keep my eyes locked on hers as I reach for my beer and lift it from the coaster. "Well we wouldn't that, would we?"

"No. We wouldn't."

I take a sip of my drink. "I appreciate the beer."

"Don't mention it."

"I don't believe you told me your name."

"Hayden."

"Hayden," I repeat.

"Yeah. You might not want to forget it, you know, since you'll be screaming it later."

I quickly glance down and try to mask my chuckle with a cough. We didn't rehearse that part. I'm pleasantly surprised and slightly impressed with my girlfriend's improvisation. Once I've collected myself, I bring my eyes back to Hayden's. She's taking a drink from her glass, also trying to hide her laugh. Then she swallows and clears her throat.

"And you are?" Hayden inquires.

"Blake."

"Right."

"Listen, *Hayden*, let me level with you here." I rest my glass on the bar and place my right hand on Hayden's knee. "As soon as we're done with our drinks here, I'm probably going to take you home with me."

"Really?"

"Really."

Hayden sets her vodka tonic beside my beer. "And why ever would you do that?"

I latch on to Hayden's suspenders and pull her closer to me. So close that I can practically taste the minty flavor of her lip balm. "Because you're kind of my type," I say in a low tone.

Hayden smiles at me. "Am I?"

I return the smile and whisper, "You are." Then I slowly brush my lips across Hayden's. She kisses me back. We lose our breaths in seconds and reluctantly pull our mouths away from one another's. We share a knowing look and exchange smiles again.

"And after all, you are my girlfriend," I add.

Hayden chuckles. "That I am."

"And also, there's that other thing."

Hayden knits her brows. We didn't rehearse this part either.

"Huh? What other thing?" She asks.

229

I reach into the front pocket of my dark blue jeggings and retrieve the copy of my house key that I had made at the locksmith's earlier that week. I take Hayden's hand in my own and pry it open. I place the silver key in her palm.

"Technically, if you want, it's our home," I say.

Hayden's eyes widen and she squeezes the key in her hand.

She grins. "I want."

I laugh. "Cool."

Hayden exhales a disbelieving snicker. "But we just made fun of Grace and Ava for U-hauling."

"Your point?"

"Blake Caruso, did you sneak off with your bestie to the locksmith?"

"No. I actually went by myself. I really didn't know Grace was going to ask Ava to move in with her. But I had already planned to offer you this key. So shiny and all."

"You seriously want to be a lesbian stereotype with me?"

"I do."

"Wow. Could you be more gay?" Hayden laughs.

I give Hayden's suspenders another tug.

"As a matter of fact, yes I can be. If you'd like, when we go home, I'll show you how."

Hayden grins slyly and takes my hand. She slides her fingers through mine. "I'd like that a lot."

I bite my bottom lip. "Oh yeah? So you're all in then?"

"Hell yes! I am so all in." Hayden beams. "Are you?"

"With you?" I lean over and steal a kiss from Hayden. "Yeah. I'm all in."

The End

230

Printed in Great Britain
by Amazon